He was only trying to warn people, but no one would listen…

"You don't understand, Mazur," Lieutenant Arnold said. "Don was influenced by your articles. He was a 'prepper' and was paranoid. You put him over the edge!"

"Hey, hey. Don't blame me for other people's problems."

Lieutenant Arnold pointed his finger at Steve menacingly. "It *is* your problem. You are the cause."

"No, I just write the facts. I don't control how readers interpret it and certainly I'm not responsibility for what do they do."

"You're wrong, Mazur. You are causing panic and chaos in our small township. Almost daily we receive phones calls about suspicious figures lurking about, about neighbors and friends and we have to look into each one."

"It seems that this Gold event is outside the serial killings just like the Dickerson murder."

"People don't see it that way. Beware the power of the word. We don't have the manpower or time to divert us from legitimate investigations." The lieutenant tossed a slip of paper on Steve's desk. "By the way, this is a ticket for a broken tail light."

"I don't have a broken light."

"You do now. Be careful what you write."

In sleepy Long Hill Township in northern New Jersey, former members of Boy Scout Troop 186 are dying decades after the Troop was disbanded. Are these deaths coincidences? Accidents? Or are they the result of something much more dubious? While the police are slow to make connections, reporter Steve Mazur, one of the remaining Scouts and a well-known conspiracy theorist, believes it is the work of one man. Steve tries to convince the surviving troop members, the local police, and anyone that will listen. As the gruesome deaths mount, township residents become frightened and alarmed by the continuing murders, and by his articles in the local newspaper. The police suspect Mazur, but can they link him to the killings before more lives are lost?

KUDOS for *The Troop*

In *The Troop* by R. James Milos, men who used to be a part of a Boy Scout troop in a small New Jersey town suddenly start dying. And no one seems to know why? One of the survivors believes it has something to do with the old Scout troop, which was disbanded decades before, and that all former members of the troop could be in danger. But he can't get anyone to believe him. The story takes us back and forth between the past events that happened in the Scout troop and the present day events happening to former Scout members—a sort of "before" and "after" look at their lives and the consequences past actions can have. The story has the feeling of a thriller, with elements of mystery and even YA—a cleverly written tale with interesting characters and plenty of surprises in the plot. What more can you ask for? ~ *Taylor Jones, Reviewer*

The Troop by R. James Milos is a story of a small-town Boy Scout troop who, when they became men, discovered that past actions and attitudes often have inadvertent consequences. When members of the former troop start being murdered many years after the troop ceased to exist, one of the men, who happens to be a reporter for the local paper, believes the murderer is focusing on the former troop members for a reason, but he doesn't know what that reason is. As he investigates, he only becomes more convinced that the killer is targeting him and his childhood friends. He also becomes the prime suspect. *The Troop* is well-written and filled with intriguing characters, unexpected twists and turns, and good-old-fashioned suspense. It will keep you turning pages from the first to the last. ~ *Regan Murphy, Reviewer*

ACKNOWLEDGEMENTS

Bethany de Barros has constantly been my biggest fan. Her encouragement kept me working toward completion. She is s true friend is every sense. Bethany and her husband PJ provided valuable editorial comments and story criticism.

Detective Jay Milos and Patrick Ackerman read the first draft; their enthusiasm was the fuel I needed to carry on. A story is only as good as its readers.

The
Troop

R. James Milos

A Black Opal Books Publication

The
Troop

Chapter 1

Homestead Park was a small subdivision in Long Hill Township, New Jersey near the Myersville Presbyterian Church—the first development of low-cost residential houses built in the 1920s. Because of its size and the few residents, it was a forgotten part of the township.

The scenic hills of the Watchung Mountains, the fascination of the Great Swamp, and the abundance of wild life and woods made for a sleepy respite for those who took the train to work in minor New Jersey cities to the east or to the end of the line, New York City.

A population of 8,800 retired each night, safely recalling picnics by the river; Memorial Day and July Fourth parades of Little Leaguers, Girl Scouts, and Boy

Scouts; restful Sundays; and crisp winter activities leading up to Christmas. It was a good place to live and raise a family. Minor traffic accidents and teenagers bored with summers created minor disruptions. The township was an extended family and these interruptions were tolerated, compared to the bustle, noise, and crimes of larger communities. And like any family, there could be contention among its members. But no one in Long Hill was prepared for what was to come, especially from one of its own.

ᏋᏍᏋᏍ

While sitting on the floor organizing abandoned belongings, he came across a beat-up tan shoe-box, wrapped with what seemed like an overabundance of black electrical tape, as if the contents of the box could escape. He didn't remember the box or ever seeing it before and wondered what was inside and if he should open it. Something—something raised his awareness and he was leery of what it might contain. The box was heavy, without any real weight, and though his curiosity was peaked, he tossed it aside and continued with other items. But it seemed to call his name. A forced glance and it appeared closer than he had thrown it. Slightly frightened, he slid over and held the box again. Nothing happened. Relieved, he tore off the tape and pulled the lid off. He thought he detected a foul odor. Inside were old Boy

Scout troop paraphernalia. Among them were a neckerchief with slide and an old yellowing paper target with three holes.

He sat on the floor with the shoe-box on his lap, fingering the fragile target. The weight of the box seemed lighter now, for things trying to be forgotten but constantly retold had crawled out and swarmed around him. He breathed in a past. Recollections, cold and moist, slithered up his neck into his head, reviving the pain and anguish so recently experienced and hid away. Despite himself, he started to remember things and events he had tried to push down since boyhood. Behind these imprisoned thoughts was a harsh, low whisper, "Harmful acts are always intentional."

He tried ignoring it now as he had through all those retellings, but he wasn't successful. Carefully built barricades started to rapidly crumble. He knew the memories would begin to apply tremendous pressure to his actions.

He started to search for the bottles of Lithium and Jack Daniels he knew were nearby, but the narrative began again and he felt himself reviewing random memories he had so much difficulty trapping and ignoring. He realized now that he had to correct what had been so he could continue without these thoughts and embarrassments trying to be heard again. He had to make amends not only for himself, but for everyone whose life had been and was diminished by bullying. Calm swept through his body and resolve gave him strength. And in this quiet revelation, he came to understand that God had given him a mission. The Troop would pay dearly for a lifetime of unforgivable scars and be a lesson for everyone else.

Boy Scout Troop 186 was a small collection of area boys: a loose bunch of thirteen and fourteen year olds not abiding by scout rules, but using scouts as a front so the All Saints' Episcopal Church in Millington, New Jersey, would provide its basement for meetings.

Kenny Richardson was a tall, lanky, dirty blond with a sharp nose. Blue eyes below bushy eyebrows were always in motion. His father was a lawyer and his family had money. He was energetic, self-assured, and willing to take up any challenge. He would do anything to be ahead of others. His family's large brown Tudor house in Millington off Valley Road was always immaculate.

Clancy Dickerson was overweight and had asthma. You knew he was around because of his constant wheezing. His forever-rosy face was round, topped by light blond hair in a bowl cut. Thanks to an allowance—a concept unfamiliar to the other boys—Clancy always had a supply of candy. He lived in a big, white-columned, federal house on the ridge along Long Hill Road in Millington and never invited anyone over. The six-acre land the seven-bedroom house sat on was manicured by Spanish workers. Clancy always wore dress shirts and pleated trousers. T-shirts, dungarees, and casual wear were for plebeians, according to his parents.

Peter Weber was dark, short, and Jewish, but he wouldn't admit to his family's religion. He denied being Jewish, even though the Troop occasionally joked about it calling him "Jew boy." He ignored it with style. He didn't want to leave the Troop, since his very best friend Paul was a part of it. Peter's family moved from New York to New Jersey and this land was a wilderness. He was always eager to please and that suited the Troop well. He never told his parents the scout meetings were in the local Episcopal Church. He walked from his bi-level to Steve's house for rides to meetings.

You had to see Paul Moody to know he was around. Paul blended in with the environment and hardly spoke. There were no distinguishing features on his face. If the police had to make a portrait of him, the results would be more like a child's simple crayon drawing. He was gentle to a point and, because of this, the Troop ignored him. His clothes were always clean and neat as if he never played outdoors. No one really knew where he lived and, at times, the boys wondered what he really was thinking. His silence scared them on occasions.

Steve Mazur's parents had divorced—something new in the early '60s and the first in the area. The neighbors, mostly his father's relatives, ignored Steve's family. The stability and reliance of his family had shattered unexpectedly for Steve. The sudden desertion by his father led Steve to believe that not everything was random. All events had meaning. So Steve didn't trust anyone and suspected all until facts were produced. JFK's assignation further strengthened this opinion. Steve sought the Troop's friendship and the opportunities to leave the house his carpenter father had built from stolen job site materials. Steve was medium height, had brown hair and pointed ears, which he was always self-conscious of. He took as a joke the sporadic "Polack" naming from the Troop as a friendly term.

Teddy Nestor was asked to be part of the Troop as a good will gesture. Teddy wasn't right. His looks were narrow and thin, as though his mother squeezed him out as quickly as possible at birth. His hair was unkempt and spiked before that was fashionable. His face was bed-sheet white. Blood apparently had difficulty making it to his brain. Teddy couldn't stand still. His arms were al-ways in motion so he looked like a scarecrow falling from his perch in a stiff wind. Thought patterns were as random as his attention span and, because of this, he was fun to be with. He sat with Troop members at the school cafeteria and was fascinating to watch. He ate entire ap-ples: core and seeds. Given a cupcake, he ate the wrapper along with the cake. He thought of the Troop as his friends. The boys thought of him as a pet and, most im-portantly, his condition made everyone in the Troop feel good about themselves. They didn't know he had mini-mal brain dysfunction. Perhaps no one knew.

Teddy lived in a 1950 wood-framed house with peel-ing lead-based paint both inside and outside. No one wanted to go inside. It was always dusty. His father was an alcoholic and everyone suspected his mother was on drugs she bartered for on the side streets in the city of Plainfield.

These boys were the core of Troop 186.

Others came and went, like Gary Wilton who was the poorest of the Troop. He was short and scruffy and wore the aroma of grease and gasoline. His knuckles contained dark dirt that matched his ragged fingernails and the greasy creases in his hands. He always looked like he needed a bath. It was easy to notice that his mother cut his hair since it was more bushy than trimmed. Gary wore faded hand-me-down clothes two generations old. The Troop thought they could use him since he lived in a car junkyard in Meyersville; all were eager to drive in a couple of years—perhaps in the junkyard before then. He didn't have scout clothes or gear, but it didn't matter to him.

Others didn't last for long, whether they didn't have money for dues, lacked appropriate scout clothing, or because of the cruel camaraderie of the group.

Since Gary and Teddy frequently joined meetings, the boys gave them discarded scout neckerchiefs and slides so they would feel part of the Troop. The boys felt noble at this generosity to their new pets. Others who didn't survive the Troop culture were quickly forgotten.

Mr. Calhoun was the Troop leader. Gray hair had started to stain his head. Horn-rimmed glasses always seemed to slip off his nose. His clothes were from the 'fifties. He favored bowties and suspenders and had a favorite tan fedora. He smelled of sour cologne. The boys didn't know why he was a scout master. They speculated that because he didn't have children maybe this role made up for it. Mr. Calhoun sadly knew the Troop wasn't interested in merit badges or American Indian traditions, and it was this knowledge that the boys used to their ends. Probably like the boys, he just wanted to belong to something.

Though he disappeared at times during meetings and outings for refreshment, the Troop always felt he was around even if it wasn't a Troop activity. He always carried a Fujica Automagic 35 mm camera and frequently asked the Troop to pose for a photo, either individually or in a group.

He was content to work with the Troop as long as they knew the scout oath and scout law. The Troop spouted each without thinking at meetings:

Scout Oath: *On my honor, I will do my best, to do my duty, to God and my country, to obey the Scout Law, to help other people at all times, and to keep myself physically strong, mentally awake, and morally straight.*

Scout Law: *A scout is trustworthy, loyal, helpful, friendly, courteous, kind, obedient, cheerful, thrifty, brave, clean, and reverent.*

cঙে৩

Arbitrary episodes that shaped his youth once again visited him and held him down as scenes of those Boy Scout days past began playing again. These indiscriminate memories once again poisoned his soul.

The Troop participated in many activities.

One summer, the Episcopal Church had a fair that consisted of home-baked goods and lemonade stands, flea market items, games for children, swirl and clown face painting, a penny toss into muffin pans, water sponge throw, and many other tame activities. The intent was not only to involve the community, but raise a little money as well.

The Troop was low on cash and needed supplies such as garbage cans and camping equipment. Mr. Calhoun encouraged the Troop to come up with an idea for the fair.

Gary volunteered a junker—a car that no amount of repair could place back on the road.

"We could have a car smash!" Blank faces told him the boys didn't know what he was talking about. "We take out all the glass and charge fifty cents to smash any part of the car with a sledge hammer. My pop will tow it over to the fair and then on to a scrap yard."

Destruction, pounding, and metal crunching—this appealed to the entire Troop.

The boys brought up the idea with Mr. Calhoun.

"I don't know boys." Mr. Calhoun emphasized his concern by rubbing the back of his neck. "It's rather violent. I don't know if the church would allow it."

The boys were ready for this. Steve explained that this was an opportunity to start earning the automotive maintenance merit badge. He was hoping he wouldn't have to concentrate on the destruction part.

"Oh, okay. I'll talk with Father Robert."

The merit badge ruse worked again.

Father Robert was reluctant at first, but because the Troop was a part of the church he agreed, as long as everything was cleaned up.

The following Saturday morning, Kenny, Clancy, Peter, Paul, Steve, and Teddy walked, bicycled, or were dropped off at Gary's small decaying white stucco ranch house. The boys waited outside, kicking the white washed tire rims lining the house front that tried to be planters and picking weeds that should have been grass. The metal on the rims had been cut and bent in an attempt to form crude flowers. Dandelions grew in the center of the rims and throughout the front yard. The lawn was unkempt and hid many small rusting car parts.

Like Clancy, Gary never invited anyone in, but Steve had been in Gary's house once. One day he'd knocked on the door to see if Gary wanted to go to the pond to torture frogs. Gary's mother answered and told Steve to come in while she called for Gary. Stark and stained walls accented the barrenness of the living room. Mustiness permeated the air. An uneven floor was polished dark brown. Steve looked closer at what kind of wood planking would do this only to discover that it was hard-packed dirt, shiny from foot ware.

While Steve's family didn't have much money, they at least had real floors. He was both shocked and pleased to learn that someone in the neighborhood was worse off than him.

Gary came rushing out of a room and quickly ushered Steve outside. Steve could see the embarrassment in his face. Steve wanted to ask a lot of questions: "Are all your floors dirt?" "Do you wipe your feet before entering?" "Do you wipe food off if you drop it?" "Do you get worms?" "Do you grow vegetables inside?"

Gary was silent. Steve told him about the day's planned activity and Gary nodded. Both walked to the pond. Gary was particularly aggressive in slicing and squashing frogs that day.

Steve wondered if Clancy had dirt floors as well, since no one had ever entered his house.

The junkyard was sprawled amidst trees in back of Gary's house. Rows and rows of cars some piled on others—canyons of metal waste. A smell of gas, oil, and grease welcomed them. Accesses were paths big enough to drive a car through the maze of wrecks. For adolescent boys, this was the place! Gary led the way.

"Which car?" Kenny asked.

"Over here, under that walnut tree—a 1947 Plymouth. The motor's out, the interior is gone, and best of all, the gas tank has been removed."

And there it was: a rusted light-green two-door beauty. Strips of chrome still ran along the bulging front fenders. A full outside visor shielded the front window that looked over a long, sleek, domed hood. The back gently sloped down, meeting two rear fenders. Almost flat dirty white sidewall tires accented the smooth configuration of the entire car. Walnut pods left dents on the roof as they fell and a thick layer of dust coated everything. All the same it looked as if it was speeding while remaining still.

Gary had a toolbox and, under his direction, the Troop began to remove all lights and windows. He started to show us how to remove the gasket around the rear window. Kenny moved to the windshield to work on it. Peter and Paul began to tear the door panels off to remove the side windows. Steve tackled the headlights.

Clancy was sitting on a tractor tire, winded from the walk.

While the boys worked, Teddy wandered off, unnoticed.

Little progress was made after a half hour in the summer sun. Steve had the headlights off and was removing a taillight when Gary became exasperated.

"Shit, this isn't getting anywhere."

All marveled at his language use.

"Let's do it the easy way."

He looked around and found a cylinder head in a pile

of parts. He heaved it at the back windshield. The tempered glass cracked as the cylinder bounced off, but remained in place.

"God damn it!" Gary retrieved the engine part and, closer to the Plymouth, threw it with both hands. The entire glass fractured into small, granular fragments.

A search began to find something to throw: a large spring, a brake drum, a timing chain, and a jack. The boys attacked the car with abandonment. Kenny threw the jack at the front windshield. Steve aimed the brake drum at the right side window. Paul pounded the left with the spring. Peter whipped the chain at the one tail light Steve hadn't removed. Clancy watched, entertained, while digging in his pocket for melted candy.

Finally the glass was gone, scattered in or around the car.

"That should to it." Gary stepped back to look at the work completed. "Nice."

"Should we clean up the glass?" Steve asked.

"No, not necessary. They ain't sharp."

"All right then, it's ready for the fair next Saturday. Let's head back."

The boys marched back up the dirt path satisfied with their accomplishment and looking forward to the weekend.

Clancy brought up the rear. Looking at the Troop in front, he realized that Teddy was absent. "Hey, anyone seen Teddy?" he called between breaths.

The group stopped and looked around as if Teddy was hiding nearby.

"We need to have that boy on a leash! Let's fan out and find him," Kenny commanded.

The troop started to take different paths into the depths of the yard when a car came barreling toward the boys.

Erratically approaching from a side path was a 1960 Ford Galaxie, veering left then right, clipping parts of stacked cars sending metal scraps into the air. Teddy was driving. Kenny stood frozen in its path. Everyone else ran for cover.

"Kenny, get out of the way!" Steve hollered from a tire pile.

At the last moment, Kenny dove right onto the dirt and the left bumper narrowly missed him.

"Teddy, you can't drive! You'll kill yourself!" Peter called uselessly from behind a Volkswagen Van as the red, square-shaped car careened by. "Jesus Christ!"

The other boys ran after the Ford passed and stopped short as it hit the Plymouth head on. The crushing sound ripped through the still summer air.

"God damn it," Peter yelled.

"Shit!" Steve moaned, mimicking Gary, clearly feeling worldly.

"Motherfucker!" Gary one-upped Steve. "That Galaxie had an automatic transmission. My pop was going to sell it."

Kenny walked slowly and joined in the lament.

"Crap! All our work!"

Everyone concentrated on the destroyed Plymouth ahead, oblivious to Teddy's condition. Moving past the Galaxie, all inspected the damage to their fair car. Without an engine, the front had folded like an accordion. It was terrible.

"Well I guess that does it," Paul said, surprising us all—not because he spoke, but for the meaning of it.

Clancy finally joined the group. "Nobody would want to beat up a wrecked car."

Everyone stood in silence with only the radiator of the Ford hissing.

"Oh my head," Teddy groaned. He had hit the steering wheel upon impact. He wasn't bleeding so there wasn't an urgent need to help him. Everyone stared disbelievingly at the crumbled cars. All the work and all the hopes were now bent and useless. Frustration pushed aside shock and was immediately replaced by anger.

"What did you do?" Kenny leaned in the car window and shouted at Teddy. "You almost killed me, you feeble moron!"

"I—I got behind the wheel to see what driving would be like. I stumped on a petal and turned the key and accidently moved the gearshift. I tried to brake it."

"Goddamn it, you ruined it for everyone! You can't drive! You can't do anything that takes brains!" Kenny raged at him.

"You probably used the gas pedal, idiot! What a re-tard!" Gary was mad at the damage and fearful of telling his father. He moved from right to left, inspecting the Galaxie, desperately hoping to find something redeeming. His face turned red and spit spewed with each invective. "What a complete moron!" He moved to the car window. "You feeble-minded shit-head! You'll pay for this!"

"Hey, no need to call names." Peter defended the Troop to this "outsider." It was okay for the Troop to razz each other, but not someone not really a part of the core group.

"Yeah, well it's not your cars!"

Kenny stepped forward. "He didn't mean it, he's just dumb."

"Doesn't matter if he meant or not, it's done. He's queer and should be locked up for everyone's safety. What a spaz!"

"Come on boys, let's get out of here." Steve turned around and walked off, feeling the Troop behind him. It was a good feeling.

Gary was left behind. It was obvious that he wasn't a part of the Troop now. Only when the boys reached the house did they realize that Teddy was left behind. It had been such a dramatic walk out that no one wanted to go back and get Teddy, so everyone waited by the road till he stumbled out of the junkyard, cradling his mid-section. His left eye was black and the back of his head was bleeding.

"What happened?" Clancy asked.

"Nothing." Teddy sounded ashamed of being beat up.

"Did Gary do this?"

"No, I hurt myself in the crash."

"Jesus Christ! Why didn't you fight back?" Kenny yelled facing Teddy. "What's' the matter with you? I'm tired of your stupidity!"

"But you weren't bleeding then," Steve replied.

"Leave me alone, just like you did before." Teddy's statement didn't register with the boys.

Peter and Paul hopped on their bicycles and headed home. Steve, Kenny, Clancy, and Teddy walked to Steve's house to telephone for a ride. Steve's mom used iodine and Band-Aid plastic strips on Teddy. She accepted a story of falling over a car part into a wall of wrecks and, with Steve, drove Teddy home. The car ride was silent.

The Troop didn't tell Mr. Calhoun what happened only that a suitable car to smash couldn't be found.

The boys fell back on the tried and true bake sale.

The Troop mothers made cookies, cupcakes, and pies and sold $34.95 worth of baked goods and the boys ate as much. Teddy, to everyone's amusement, ate four cupcakes, wrappers included. There was just enough money to buy two shiny garbage cans, a pot, and a pan.

Kenny wasn't visibly mad at Teddy anymore, but kept his distance and, when he could, threw barbs and taunts at him. It made Kenny feel good.

Gary was absent at school for a while with a broken arm. His father didn't take the Galaxie news well.

Chapter 2

The back yard of Steve's house ran up to a sloping field. In the winter, at the top of the field, members of the Troop went sledding. They built the best sledding paths in the state.

From the top of the hill to the bottom of the front yard, the path ran a good mile in their eyes. By hauling water in pails up the hill, the boys could wet the track down so it would be icy. In fact, it became so icy and slick that the boys reached speeds of up to sixty miles an hour. And these speeds were verified. Steve brought his father's measuring stick from a carpenter's toolbox. Unfolding the stick, Steve laid out twenty feet, five times. Clancy stood at the hundred-foot mark blotting his constantly running nose with a coat sleeve.

Kenny would shout "Go" and launch himself down the path.

Clancy counted in thousands: one, one thousand...two, one thousand...three, one thousand..." He stopped counting as a sled went by. Kenny passed at the four, one thousand mark. Steve took a turn and reached three, one thousand.

All the Troop needed to do now was figure out how fast they went by applying a few math principles they thought they knew. The speedometer on a car measured how fast a car went by time and mileage: sixty miles an hour meant one mile per minute—sixty minutes in an hour—and one half mile per second—sixty seconds in a minute. So by counting the seconds it took to go a measured hundred feet, they could accurately determine speed. There were 5,280 feet in a mile—and there were about fifty-two 100s in a mile. So a count of four seconds for one hundred feet gave them two hundred and eight seconds for a full mile—four time fifty-two—they divided this by sixty seconds in minute for three-point-five. They then divided three-point-five by sixty minutes for point-oh-fifty-eight.

And finally they divided point-of-fifty-eight by one hundred feet and discovered that Kenny was traveling at fifty-eight miles per hour in that measured run! The math was complicated, but thanks to public schooling, it was figured it out to the boy's pleasure.

"Neat! Is there a math merit badge?" asked Peter.

No one knew. They would have to bring it up with Mr. Calhoun.

They built two ramps. The path took a wide S pattern with the first ramp in the middle of the S. It then straightened out for run over the embankment in Steve's backyard. This was where a second ramp was placed. Like the first, it was just two feet high, but with the added drop of the bank, it really was five feet high. The trail then passed between Steve's house on the right and Uncle Franous's house near the road.

A necessary hard right at bottom ended in the dirt ditch to avoid Meyersville Road.

Canning wax was rubbed on sled runners to make them extra fast. The sled was handed to Gary.

"You go first," Kenny demanded as he thrust the sled toward Gary.

Gary looked suspicious, but took the sled and began to pigeon-walk to the top of the snowy hill. He hoisted the American Eagle sled on his back till it became too difficult to carry then pulled it the remaining way.

The sled track glistened in spots where it was watered. It was fast. So fast that one could lose control and spin out.

Gary wasn't afraid of crashing; to walk down would have been unthinkable.

He stood behind the sled, took a deep breath, and threw himself to the ground. He was rocketing toward the first turn—his nose inches from the frozen ground. He was going so fast he didn't see the first ramp and didn't enjoy the brief flight. Upon impact with the track, the air was pushed out of Gary's lungs and his head hit the front metal hinge of the sled. His vision was blurred from the cold air and the bump. He dragged his boot toes to slow down and thought about rolling off but didn't want to appear weak. The second curve held him to the track by gravity. He was headed toward the final ramp. He hung on with the bravery of youth, gripped the wooden steering handle, and rose into the air, immediately colliding with a snow wall.

He went through it, off the sled, rolled, and landed against a tree.

His hat was off. Snow was in his ears, nose, and mouth. His eyes were frozen shut. His back ached. For a moment, he didn't know where he was. He blew snow from his nose and spat it from his mouth. He took off his mittens and used a pinky to dig it from his ears. Gary heard music, but as more snow was removed laughter filled in.

Kenny, Clancy, Peter, and Steve all were pleased at Gary's crash. They had erected a frozen snow wall at the end of the ramp.

"You really hit it and went head over heels in the air!"

"Man did you look funny!"

Gary, once again, felt like a fool for having been deceived. Someday they would all pay for their meanness.

eↄeↄ

One January weekend, Mr. Calhoun reserved a cabin on Bass River State Forest in Southern New Jersey. Late Friday night, the Troop crowded into Mr. Calhoun's Jeep Patriot and headed out for Tuckerton.

Bass River State Forest was the first land purchased by the State of New Jersey in 1905 for public recreation. The sixty-seven acre Lake Absegami within the park was dug in the 'thirties for water activities. Oddly, Absegami meant "little water" in Algonquin. The Troop had plans to ice fish.

It was dark upon arrival. After fumbling with knapsacks, sleeping bags, and gear, lighting a fire within the large damp wooden cabin was the first priority. Fortunately, the park supplied ample wood. All the boys had earned the Fire Safety Merit Badge, except for Teddy. The badge was given to him without his touching a match. The Troop didn't feel safe trusting Teddy with fire. Using Scout skills, the flue was checked to make sure it was opened. Tinder was placed in the hearth with wood splinters on top. The tinder was lit and allowed to burn before small logs were crossed on top, followed by larger split wood as the fire progressed.

The only problem with fireplaces was that, while they gave warmth near the hearth, the air was sucked from other areas, which became cold so the race for the beds nearest the fire began as soon as the boys entered the cabin. Kenny claimed the closest, Peter and Paul obtained beds next to each other, followed by Steve, Clancy, and Teddy. Actually Teddy wasn't last, but Clancy threw Teddy's sleeping bag from the third bed to the last one in back of the room.

"Hey!" Teddy managed to protest.

Clancy stood next to him and stared. "What?"

It felt good to have someone lower on the totem pole. "Nothing."

A quick stop at McDonald's before arriving had eliminated the need to prepare supper.

"Let's tell stories," Steve suggested. "I'll go first."

It was a story everyone except Teddy had experienced before and anticipation was high. The Troop sat near the hearth, anticipating what would happen. Mr. Calhoun was off somewhere.

"A long time ago, in the eighteen hundreds, and right around here, was a wealthy farmer. He bought a new McCormick reaper. One day, he was out in his wheat field when the blades of the reaper froze. He stopped his two horses and went around back to investigate. A rock had become stuck between the cutting edges. As he dislodged the stone, horseflies landed on one horse and began to bite. Startled, the horse moved forward cutting off the right arm of the farmer. It was a mess: blood everywhere, the limb on the ground. Holding his stump, the farmer raced to the farmhouse, calling out his wife's name. Well, he reached the house and they went to a doctor. They couldn't save the arm because the technology wasn't there in the eighteen hundreds.

"Now, because he was vain and rich, he commissioned a golden arm to wear. It was a beautiful thing, all bright and shiny and rigged with leather straps attached to his shoulder. He became the talk of the county. Soon his tale spread throughout all of New Jersey and beyond.

"He wore it with pride. When he died, he willed that his arm be buried with him. The funeral was big and everyone attended.

"Among the mourners, however, was a thief. Later that night, the thief went back to the cemetery with a shovel and pry bar. Working by lantern light, he dug down in the still-loose dirt to the coffin, opened it, and ripped the golden arm from the farmer. Not even bothering to fill the grave in, he rushed home to his wife and went upstairs to the bedroom.

"'Where have you been?' she asked.

"'Making us rich,' he replied, placing a bundle under the bed.

"'What do you mean?'

"'Never mind, just go to sleep.'

"Sleep never came for, as they shut their eyes, they heard the front door open.

"'What was that?' the wife asked.

"'The wind.'

"Then they both heard footsteps on the stairs and a low moan: 'Who stole my golden arm?'

The wife sat up grabbing her husband.

"Closer the footsteps sounded and louder the phrase, 'Who stole my golden arm?'"

Steve stood and, with a flashlight under his chin, approached each scout. "'Who stole my golden arm?' The footsteps were near the top and the moan was in anger. 'Who stole my golden arm?' The frightened couple huddled together afraid of what could be behind the bedroom door."

As Steve went to each boy, his voice became more eerie. "'Who stole my golden arm?'"

Steve neared Teddy and moved within a foot of Teddy's face. "'Who stole my golden arm?'" The flashlight bathed Steve's face in shadows and light. Steve grinned, gave a wide stare, and again asked, "'Who stole my golden arm?'

"*You did*!" he yelled suddenly and pointed at Teddy's face.

The abruptness of the act and the finger pointing caused Teddy to reel backward off his chair and hit his head on the floor.

Everyone laughed at the expected result, everyone except Teddy, who gradually stood and sat back in the chair, embarrassed and hurt.

Mr. Calhoun appeared. He was pleased the boys were having a good time based on their laughter, but now had to announce that it was bedtime.

Tomorrow would be ice fishing.

"The trick to good sunny side-up eggs is fresh eggs and bacon fat. Fry the bacon first, and then crack the eggs into the left over bacon fat," Mr. Calhoun instructed in the morning. After a satisfying breakfast, everyone dressed in warm layered clothing. Teddy wore a Salvation Army hooded jacket. His face was almost lost in the faux fur of the hood. Steve was happy in winter. Wool head gear concealed his ears unlike baseball caps in more temperate weather.

Mr. Calhoun sent them out fishing while he tended to "scout master activities."

There was a crispness in the air. The landscape looked like vanilla icing. Snow squealed underneath as the boys walked the short distance to Lake Absegami, steering Teddy to keep him from wandering off because of his limited vision.

The Troop didn't have a shanty and had little ice fishing equipment. What they did have were plastic buckets for seating, fishing poles, and a long-handled blade, called a spud, for opening a hole in the ice. The Troop slid on the ice till reaching a spot not far from shore. They took turns pounding the ice with the spud, finally opening two good sized ragged holes four inches deep to the lake below. Hooking bright red lures to their fishing lines, the boys sat around the openings, jiggling the lines to attract fish.

Teddy was the best at this since he couldn't stop his arms from moving.

"Should have brought cardboard so our feet wouldn't be on the ice," Peter lamented after an uneasy hour on the bucket, rubbing one foot then the other for warmth.

"Teddy, run back to the cabin and get us some cardboard," Steve commanded.

Teddy hesitated, wanting to be part of the Troop, but not its constant lackey.

"Come on Teddy!" Kenny urged.

Teddy put his pole on the ice and slowly moved toward the lake bank, but not in the direction they had arrived. No one noticed.

A stream fed into the lake where Teddy was walking. Beneath the snow, the ice had turned from blue to gray. This running water made the ice thinner than the lake body.

Teddy heard a loud crack and froze. An inch break had opened in front of him.

Fearfully he yelled, "Help!"

The distance, the wind, and the warm wrappings and hats on the Troop's heads prevented them from hearing.

Teddy didn't want to turn around. He shouted till his voice turned to screams, watching the fracture, hoping it didn't grow.

"Help me! Please help me!" Teddy now saw the crack creeping toward him very slowly.

"Where is that clown Teddy?" Peter asked after

twenty minutes went by. "He should be back by now."

"Can't trust him to anything. He's like a child," Paul muttered.

Clancy stood up and looked around, finally spotting Teddy near the distant lake shore. "What's he doing?"

The others followed Clancy's pointing.

"He's not moving! Something must be up."

The Troop moved toward him. Paul grabbed the spud and followed. The Troop arrived within a few feet of Teddy.

"What's up?"

"What's the matter?"

Inquiries were ended with another loud crack.

"The ice is cracking!" Teddy shouted. "Are you idiots?"

The Troop was more shocked by Teddy's demeanor than the cracking ice.

Clancy finally caught up. The sounds increased.

"All right. Everybody down and slide away from Teddy. Clancy get back," Kenny ordered.

The Troop gently lowered to the lake surface, pivoted around, and slid on their stomachs a safe distance from Teddy.

"What do we do now?" asked Paul.

"Who weighs less?" Kenny inquired. "You, Paul, and you have the spud. Slide back to Teddy and push the spud in front of you. Teddy, lay down and grab the spud."

Paul slid toward Teddy till the spud was within

reach. Teddy clutched it. The others lay flat on the ice in a row, each holding the foot in front except for Clancy, who now pulled. Slowly the line moved away from the lake bank.

Every one lay still till the fright passed then slowly stood up. Carefully and silently, the Troop went back to the fishing hole and packed up.

No one said anything. Each was still shaky. Only Clancy's wheezing at the unexpected physical exertion could be heard.

After a subdued supper, Mr. Calhoun left the cabin. There were mutterings about the trouble Teddy always caused and the fact that he didn't thank anyone for the rescue. Teddy left the table early and went to his bunk, pulling the covers over his head.

For the rest of the weekend, Teddy stayed away from the others, even when they invited him in on a snowball fight. He was on a slow learning curve. He took off his neckerchief and stuffed it into his knapsack.

ᘿᔕᘿᔕ

Slights and bullying didn't end with an incident. They were carried through life and affected others as well others as well. He was proof of this and he knew only one way he could end it—or else it would never end.

ᘿᔕᘿᔕ

The Myersville Presbyterian Church sold Christmas trees every year. Steve's father was a ruling elder of the church and ran the affair. The church never knew or never wanted to know that his father abused his children and wife. He was too good a leader. Even after the messy divorce, the church chose him before his family.

Mr. Calhoun volunteered the Troop to assist in selling the trees to earn a Salesmanship Merit Badge.

The pine trees were stacked in near the back of the church parking lot. White light bulbs were strung on wire supported by poles on two-by-four constructed stands, which Steve's father had built.

A colorful decorated tree with bright lights and ornaments stood prominently in front of the rows of naked trees to lure customers in.

Steve enjoyed talking with men about a variety of things—as if he was a grownup. Idle discussions included driving in and out of the same rain storm on the same highway, could you eat grass, and other meaningless topics, just to pass the time till the next tree buyer appeared. He also appreciated this time when his father was on good behavior.

Steve quickly learned a sales pitch about the different types of trees and how they should be trimmed. The blue to dark green Douglas fir had a natural pyramidal shape and a long life after cutting. The Fraser fir was very fragrant and its slender profile fit into small rooms.

For excellent needle retention, the Scotch pine was

the most popular. Remove branches from the trunk to allow room when placing in the tree stand. Cutting an inch off the trunk removed the sappy seal that formed from the initial cut and allowed water uptake for longevity.

One snowy evening, Mr. Calhoun arrived. He brought with him Gary and a boy Steve didn't know. He was small, dark, and kept his eyes down.

"I've brought Gary and a new Scout to help out," Mr. Calhoun announced to no one in particular. "This is Giovanni Baglio."

"Does he speak English?" Kenny asked.

"Of course, he does." Mr. Calhoun then left to talk with the other men.

Gary ambled over to Steve to find out what he should do. Steve explained the prices, variety of trees, and how best to sell them. Giovanni stood alone lost amid a sea of green and blue pines.

Periodically during the night, Steve's father would check the money taken in.

At nine o'clock, he discovered all the money was missing from the lock box on the steps to the church. He quickly called all the men together.

"Did anyone take the proceeds?"

"What do you mean," asked one.

"The money is gone. The lock box is empty!"

All looked at each other, unwilling to even think that one of them was a thief.

The 'locked' box wasn't locked?" another church member inquired.

"No. We were always making change and this is a church, for Christ sake!" Steve's father replied as if he was home.

Everyone looked at the other.

Pastor William stepped forward and took the cash box from Steve's father. "I'm sure that whoever took it was in need and that is the mission of this church—to serve the needy and poor. Let us forget this and move forward. I will take charge of the box."

"I bet that wop took it," Kenny whispered to Clancy,

Behind a tree row, Giovanni heard the remark and set off walking home.

So the night went on until eleven o'clock when everyone went home.

"Anyone see Giovanni?" Mr. Calhoun shouted.

No one answered.

Mr. Calhoun picked up Giovanni for the next Scout meeting. He didn't mention the Christmas tree sale or Giovanni's absence.

After a half hour, Giovanni asked Mr. Calhoun to take him home because of a stomach ache. The Troop had looked at him with frowning faces and whispered behind his back. He had had enough.

The thief was never discovered.

Chapter 3

The Great Swamp National Wildlife Refuge was an interesting place for boys to roam, fish, and skate. Its area was the size of Long Hill Township and contained fox, deer, muskrat, turtles, fish, frogs, mosquitoes, ticks, deer, a wide variety of wildflowers, dragon flies and other insects, and more than 224 species of birds. The Port Authority of New York and New Jersey had plans to turn the Great Swamp into a major regional airport to supplement Newark Airport's ability to accommodate large jet aircraft.

Residents of Long Hill collected donations, purchased 2,600 acres, and gave the land to the federal government for a national wildlife refuge. The National Park Service designated the Great Swamp as a registered National Natural Landmark. The eastern half of the Refuge was designated as a wilderness by Congress—the first wilderness area within the Department of the Interior.

To the boys, the Swamp was a great place to explore and get away from adult supervision.

The edge of the Swamp was north, just outside of Meyersville, and yards off Meyersville Road. In the winter, it offered small areas for skating around eight-inch mounds of wetland grass. The depth of the frozen water was minimal, so falling through only meant wet pants. Used skates could be bought at Arnie's Resale Shop near the grassy center of the village for only four dollars. Steve, Peter, Paul, Gary, and Teddy made yearly trips to the shop, sometimes trading their old pairs for sturdy leather hockey skates. Kenny and Clancy always sported new Tackaberry skates. On the rare days that Giovanni joined them, he slid on the ice with street shoes.

The boys would chase each other or attempt to play "swamp hockey" using sticks and a rock till they tired-out. They rested on the mounds. On especially cold days, they set the dry grass on fire, trying to get warm. It usually burned out before adequate heat was attained, but the lure of fire was too fascinating to a group of young boys.

At sunset one day, someone came up with the idea of creating torches so they could squeeze in more skating. The dried out grass was tightly wrapped around the end of branches, tied together with cattail strips, and lit. They paraded through the swamp.

Sparks and flaming grass fell from the torches.

Giovanni wasn't as fast and followed the best he could, slipping and sliding.

The skate line turned with Kenny leading the way. As darkness increased, the torch lights decreased. The line headed back toward Giovanni whose poorly constructed torch was no longer providing illumination. As Giovanni looked for a suitable location to place the branch so no one trip on it, Kenny crashed into him and the others into the ones in front.

All fell to the ice, most torches scattered across the marsh.

Giovanni screamed.

"Jesus, Grease Ball, it wasn't that bad," Kenny reprimanded as he got up.

"My face, my face!"

Kenny picked up his sputtering torch and positioned it near Giovanni's head. The glowing torch had hit Baglio's cheek and left a nasty burn.

"Crap!"

"What happened?" Peter asked

"Gio's face is burned."

Peter chipped ice from the edge of a grass mound and placed the swampy slab on the cheek.

"Well, it wouldn't have happened if he knew how to build a proper torch and had the money to at least buy used skates so he could keep up with us."

Gary looked at Kenny and, in the newly born night,

understood the aura of Kenny's self-concern—and not for the last time.

The incident was soon forgotten, except by Giovanni Baglio, who would forever feel branded as inferior.

He tried three more Scout meetings, but kept hearing "guinea" and "grease ball." Hardly any of the Troop, except for Gary, interacted with him. No one, not even Mr. Calhoun, commented on the scar. He did not fit.

He told the Scout Master that he was needed at work. Mr. Calhoun easily accepted the excuse. Giovanni silently cursed the man for allowing all this to happen.

ತಿಞ್ಞ

In the spring, the boys gradually came around to their next non-scouting activity. They would meet and throw rocks into the Millington Gorge—something not sanctioned by parents or the scout leader.

The Millington Gorge started at the beginning of the Passaic River. Over 10,000 years ago, drainage from the Glacial Lake Passaic, now the Great Swamp, cut through the western Watchung Hills and carved a deep liquid path. The steep forty-five-degree-or-more cliffs on either side were covered with eastern redbud, birch, hickory, and dogwood trees with thick brush growing where the sunlight fought to illuminate the ground. The dirt Pond Hill Road on the right edge of the gorge, opposite the National Gypsum Plant, was a "shortcut" to Valley Road and Stirling. It didn't have a crossing signal where it ran over the train tracks. The unfortunate either didn't hear the train whistle or thought they could beat the train over the tracks, were crushed in their cars, and usually dragged some two hundred feet down the track.

There wasn't a bank to the river. The land just folded into it. While it is a New Jersey geographical wonder and a great place to explore, it was also a dangerous place.

Steve remembered his mother, Thelma, telling a story about driving on Pond Hill. Today, as back in the 'thirties, there were no guard rails. Thelma's boyfriend had a little too much to drink at the party they had just attended. It was late, nine o'clock, and Thelma was worried what her mother would do when she came home at this hour. Her boyfriend leaned over to kiss her. Thelma resisted and, in the tussle, the car veered left over the edge and slid down twenty feet. It was prevented from tumbling into the Passaic River by five maple saplings. The two managed to slip out of the vehicle and climb up the bank. It was pitch black as they walked the dirt road toward the trestle to find help. Ahead a dim light shown. It was from a decaying gray wooden house. They knocked on the door, and an old black man answered. Thelma was afraid. Her boyfriend explained what had happened. A telephone call for a tow truck was placed. The two sat in the poorest house Thelma had ever been in on a ragged couch for one hour, waiting for the truck to arrive, with another hour and a half to pull it successfully onto the road. It was still in serviceable condition, though it had a few dents on the left side. At twelve o'clock, Thelma stepped though her front door and was relieved that her mother had gone to bed. This time, the gorge let them live.

Thelma would not be happy if she knew Steve was at the gorge. It held bad memories for her, therefore, she thought it was an evil place.

And the gorge could be a frightening place. Steve didn't know how deadly it would be. But in the daytime it held wonders for a group of young boys.

One of these wonders was the ninety-foot-long Erie Lackawanna train trestle spanning the river. No safety rails, just one track on massive black beams supported by three concrete stanchions. High schoolers had crept on the narrow side to spray paint slogans and names, becoming famous and admired throughout the school. The boys weren't that brave.

The neighborhood band met there, not as Scouts, but as a troop of boys fishing the Passaic, looking for Lenape Indian signs, or, most often, searching for flat rocks or debris to drop into the river from the edges of the trestle. The explosion of the hit was loud and exciting. No one thought of oncoming trains.

National Gypsum situated its plant above the gorge near the trestle. It made sheet rock and wallboards. Environmental laws were loose in the 'sixties and the company would throw defective gypsum board and waste products on the ridge above the river. It seemed as if the back bays of the plant were vomiting into the gorge. Weather and gravity moved the rubble down to a location that the boys could easily reach in their search for something to drop.

The slope was steep and slippery, with molding debris wedged against trees and precariously lying on the ground. Some had made it to the river. Slowly dissolving white drywall pieces were visible below the surface. The Passaic started to spoil here.

"See that?" Steve pointed to the gypsum board strewn slope. "That's because the government is in collusion with corporations. They are ruining the environment and nobody cares."

"Jesus, there's a good size piece to drop." Peter ignored Steve's usual rant and held onto a slender dogwood tree trunk as he indicated a board near the top that had been recently discarded so it wasn't soft or moldy. "It's three quarter inch! Gary, go for it," he urged.

"I don't know, it looks unsafe," Paul commented. He was half way up the edge of the loose packed rubble.

"Go for it, Gary."

"Come on, you can do it!"

The rest of the boys egged him on, except for Clancy who couldn't make it up the hill. He had good reason to disapprove of the way the Troop treated Gary, but remained silent for he had few friends. Gary looked toward Paul, then the others. Fear and the desire to fit in competed. He began to scramble up the hill in the middle of the rubbish toward the three-quarter-inch wallboard.

Kenny whispered to Peter and they both yelled out: "Snake! Snake, Gary, look out for the snake!"

Gary jumped back and landed on gypsum board that slid underneath him. He fell on a large piece and started a slide down the hill.

Peter laughed with the others at the sight. "Gary's going for a toboggan ride in summer."

The board hit a tree and turned sideways. Gary rolled off, tumbled, and went head first into the river.

"Can Gary swim?" Steve asked.

No one knew, but Gary did float, his spring jacket waving with the current. Clancy positioned himself on the bank and grabbed Gary's hair.

"Ow!" Gary cried between mouthfuls of river.

Clancy dragged him through thickets to dry ground. Everyone gathered around him and patted his back. The fat boy finally did some good.

"That was neat!"

"Nice slide, junk boy."

"Fun ride, hey?"

Gary stood, dripping from his head, shirt, and trousers to his sneakers. He was not looking or talking to anyone. Not for the first time, he kept the anger bottled.

e/se/s

Without knowing, he had crumpled the target. Escaped memories were eating his existence. He squeezed his fists and face in an effort to defend himself. Did he forget to take Lithium this week? After years of therapy, he had buried his adolescence and now it returned, itching, biting, and digging into his conscience.

He took deep breaths and released the target. He gave into the hidden memories and allowed them to come home again.

Chapter 4

Mr. Calhoun had secured permission one autumn to hunt on the Early Estate on Schooley's Mountain, twenty minutes north of Millington. There wasn't a hunting merit badge, but the Troop would use this to "earn" the cooking, rifle, and shotgun shooting badges. It made Mr. Calhoun very happy.

It was the Scouts' job to organize the hunt.

The Troop put Teddy in charge of the two steel garbage cans bought from the bake sale at the church. Ostensibly, the Troop hoped this responsibility would help him, but really because none of the boys wanted to be bothered with the cans. The boys gathered Wednesday night to arrange the weekend hunt. The church provided storage space. Everyone moved through the closets for pots, pans, utensils, brooms, and other cleaning materials—everything needed for a cabin in the woods weekend, but found the metal garbage cans missing. Teddy lost them! The boys searched the church basement and questioned Teddy till he became upset. No explanation for their absence was forthcoming. That was Teddy.

"Christ, were did you put them?" Peter exclaimed. He always brought up Jesus as much as possible.

"I don't know!" Teddy looked ready to cry now. His eyes began watering and his hands were white, balled into fists.

The Troop accepted his mistake and bought a plastic can along with two days provisions allowing one night for hunter's stew.

The Early Estate was twenty-five acres atop Schooley's Mountain. At the end of a field, in back of the large manor house, was a small cabin. Friday evening Mr. Calhoun parked along the driveway. With personal items, shotguns, and supplies, the boys made two hikes from the car to the cabin before settling in.

Steve secured a top bunk bed. Teddy was below. Mr. Calhoun was at the big house visiting.

As the sun set and darkness took over, all went to bed for a morning hunt. The cabin had two rows of three bunk beds and a small room with a single bed. Steve had soaked some old socks in warm water and slightly wrung them out.

"Teddy. Teddy, I feel sick," Steve called to the bunk below.

Everyone was awake and attentive.

"What?" Teddy replied?

Steve waited for the moment.

"What?" Teddy stuck his head out to look up.

Steve made vomiting noises and dropped the wet socks onto Teddy's upturned face.

Teddy screamed, rolled out of the bed onto the floor. He staggered up and raced outside to the pump. On the way, he bumped into the kitchen table which made a horrible scream as it slid along the wood floor. This caused another outburst of laughter.

Teddy was fun.

Mr. Calhoun and Teddy didn't go hunting with us. The scout leader was most likely afraid to be in the woods with thirteen year olds with loaded shotguns. Teddy was too noisy. Game would flee at the sounds he made thrashing through the woods. He was left at the cabin with a minor chore of raking leaves, and the promise to teach him how to shoot later.

Kenny had a Mossberg 500 12 gauge pump—the envy of the Troop. It was new, had a vent rib barrel and twin sites. It was a beauty. The rest had hand-me-downs from grandfathers, fathers, and brothers. Steve's father left him nothing and his brother wasn't a hunter, so the only gun his mother could afford was a single shot J.C. Penny .410 bore. This was the smallest shotgun gauge.

He hid his embarrassment by claiming it was more difficult to hit something with fewer pellets. This might have
been true as he rarely shot anything.

"You know the government is secretly trying to take
our guns away by attacking the NRA," Steve said to no
one in particular. "The government is more involved in
our lives than we think."

As usual, he was ignored.

Gary was along this time for the outing. He had an
old side-by-side 12 gauge that looked like it was from the
1800s or, as Kenny suggested, from a trash pile. His arm
was bent. There wasn't money for a doctor and his father
had strapped short pieces of wood around the break. It
healed in time, but wasn't the same. The car smash was
never brought up.

Peter didn't own a gun. His parents said they had
seen enough violence to last a lifetime. The boys really
didn't know what that meant. He went with the Troop as
a "spotter."

They lost sight of Paul as soon as they entered the
woods.

The boys hunted all day Saturday and came back
with a rabbit and two squirrels.

Leaves were scattered in the grass, some actually in
small piles. Teddy had worked on raking.

As usual, Mr. Calhoun was at the manor.

Peter and Paul took the game out back to skin and
butcher. Butcher was the key word. No one had taught

them how to prepare game. Butchering wasn't in the Scouts' agenda.

Steve placed a large pot on the wood burning stove, added water, potatoes, carrots, onions, and assorted spices bought some time ago. He sprinkled it all in hoping to mask the gaminess. The butchered carcasses were brought in. You could only recognize the rabbit from the squirrels by the size of the hind quarters. The bloody pieces went into the pot. The stew liquid turned brown and, as it boiled, fluorescent bubbles rose and released an awful smell. By mutual consent, the supper was deemed ready to eat. Steve scooped out ladles full of stew making sure each had a piece of meat.

If Mr. Calhoun was present the boys would attempt a grace, but without him each inserted a spoon in the dark mixture—except Paul, who said a silent prayer. The Troop was used to his religious attitude and tolerated it. Everyone ate the vegetables, but were reluctant to eat the meat. Only Gary enjoyed it without hesitation, as if he ate something like it every day. Everyone commented that it was because Gary ate rats from the junk yard and skunks under the house. Gary put his spoon down and refused to eat anymore.

"Teddy, how's the game?" Kenny asked, moving on to the next victim.

"Yeah, is it good?" Clancy followed.

Teddy picked out a squirrel hind leg. Everyone watched intently as he looked it over.

"Eat it Teddy," Peter urged.

Steve joined the throng. "It's good!"

Teddy sniffed the reddish puckered meat and looked around the room. The boys all smiled encouragingly. Then he bit into it and ripped the forest protein off the bone. Everyone looked for signs of disgust. Nothing. Teddy sat there and chewed on the squirrel.

Forgetting that Teddy would eat most anything, the Scouts grabbed chunks and proceeded to eat. It was disgusting!

Paul quietly gagged into a napkin then neatly folded it on his paper plate.

Peter opened his mouth and let the chewed meat fall. "This tastes like miltz!" Realizing he had spoken in Yiddish, he mumbled, "I'm going to wash up," and raced to the pump outside.

The rest threw out the meat with vocal gags and choking gestures.

Teddy finished his squirrel leg in silence. Steve thought he detected a smile as Teddy watched the boys have a little taste of their own medicine.

After everyone was settled down and Peter came sheepishly back, Clancy came to the rescue. Dipping into his knapsack, he produced Ring Dings, Ding Dongs, and Moon Pies. Along with the packed envelopes of Kool-Aid, the hunter's dinner turned into a feast.

Crazy Eights and Hi Low card games were played before the Scouts turned in.

Tomorrow the boys were going to teach Teddy how to shoot and have fun with it.

Later that night, wine and cigar odors announced the return of Mr. Calhoun.

In the morning, all gathered around Mr. Calhoun as he mumbled something about God, life, youth, and piety. No one really listened, though Gary seemed attentive. It was enough to report back to the church that there was a service on Sunday.

After a breakfast of scrambled eggs and crispy bacon cooked by the scout leader, the group went out to a clear autumn day.

Kenny had brought his much coveted Remington bolt action single shot synthetic stocked .22 rifle. It was a smooth Mohawk brown with white mother-of-pearl inlays. The pistol grip made it exceptionally attractive. This was the highlight of the camping trip in more ways than one.

To the right and in back of the cabin was a pile of downed trees. This would be a great backstop since a .22 bullet could travel up to a mile and a half. The boys were cautious and placed more fallen logs from the woods to ensure safety.

A hand-made target was tucked under the bark. The group moved to what was thought to be a good distance. A chair and a blue bench from the cabin to steady aim were placed before the target.

Kenny made a show of placing a bullet in the barrel.

He kneeled behind the bench and sighted. The crisp crack was pleasant to hear. Kenny missed the target completely. Some were pleased, but kept the emotion to themselves as each waited a turn to shoot.

All had a chance to shoot. None of the boys hit the target, except for Steve and Gary who came close to the bull's eye. Teddy was invited to stand by the bench for a turn as the boys had promised. Paul used his stealth skills and disappeared into the cabin. Teddy wouldn't miss him. He was too excited about the shoot.

Kenny loaded the rifle and explained the proper way to sight. Peter stepped behind Teddy and, in a serious tone reminded him of the distance a bullet could travel. If he didn't hit the target or the logs it might kill someone beyond the field.

"Take your time, Teddy. Be careful," was his final admonition.

Everyone cautiously watched Teddy try to hold the rifle still. It looked like another limb since it moved from left to right, then right to left. His knuckles were white from squeezing. His hair waved in the slight breeze. If a scare crow could drop from his cross and take up a fire-arm, this was a near as possible.

"Sit down on the grass and use the bench to steady your aim," Steve suggested.

Teddy fell to one knee. The barrel swiveled around in the boy's direction. All flopped to the ground in fear.

Teddy smiled. "What?"

"Keep pointing the rifle at the logs, not us!" Clancy yelled.

Teddy turned, placed the .22 on the bench, and sat behind it.

Only now did anyone realize what was happening.

"Maybe we should take the .22 away from Teddy," Kenny whispered.

"No, let him shoot. Everything is set up," Clancy replied.

Teddy eyed along the sights. The rifle didn't move for a full minute. Crack, he fired.

The noise was the cue for Paul. He came rushing out of the cabin with ketchup on his face and hands. "I've been shot!" he screamed.

Teddy's face became whiter. "Oh no!" He stood, looked at Paul, and in a panic ran toward the road.

Everyone chuckled at the effect the prank had on Teddy, without realizing he hadn't stopped running.

"That was good."

"Nice job Paul, you almost scared me."

"All right!"

"That was neat!"

All verbally patted each other's back.

The boys started to clean up before Mr. Calhoun came back. Paul went to the water pump to wash the ketchup off. Others brought the chair and bench in. Steve retrieved the target. It had a hole in the bull's eye. Teddy hit the center! "Hey guys look at this!"

He showed the target to everyone.

"Wow!"

"He was better than all of us!"

"Teddy!" all shouted.

And it was then that all realized his absence.

"Jesus Christ! He ran toward the road," Peter shout-ed, pumping his arm, finger pointed to Schooley's Moun-tain Road. "But now I don't see him."

"Should we go after him?" Paul seemed to be talking to himself.

Silence padded the air as the Troop thought instead of reacting.

"He'll come back," someone finally said.

It was easy to dismiss minor problems.

All began packing Troop supplies and personal be-longings for an afternoon departure home.

The Troop Leader came back and opened the gate to his Jeep Patriot.

Everything was stuffed in, leaving room in the back for Teddy. The Jeep held a driver and two passengers in the front seat, three in the back seat, and Teddy in the rear.

"Make sure everything is out of the cabin and that it's in good shape," Mr. Calhoun called out.

Paul was nearest and went in for a survey. He came out holding a full plastic can.

"Why wasn't the garbage emptied?"

"It's Teddy's job," Paul whispered.

"And where is Teddy?"

Everyone looked around as if this was the first time they realized he was gone. The Scout Law didn't mention lying and no one really knew what trustworthy meant so all faked ignorance.

"All right, spread out and look for him."

The Troop fanned out toward the field and woods shouting his name, hoping that he really might be near. After a useless half hour, the boys returned to the cabin and Mr. Calhoun.

"When is the last time someone saw him?"

Steve took this as an out and replied, "Maybe he took a walk to the general store."

"Lock the cabin and get in the car. We'll ride to the store."

The Schooley's Mountain General Store was established in 1830 and had not grown since. It was a small red building with a pot stove in the middle of the one room inside, a wheel of cheddar cheese on a barrel on a wooden counter in the back, along with a bronze mechanical cash register. Candy and canned goods were on wall shelves. It was two miles from the Early Estate. As the Jeep slowly drove, everyone searched the road side and woods for any sign of Teddy. At the store, Kenny went in and came out shaking his head.

"Teddy wasn't here."

Fear set in. Quietly all thought, *Not again*! *How could he do this to us for a second time*?

Mr. Calhoun became agitated. To his knowledge, he had never lost a scout before. "All right, all right, calm down. We'll ride around, looking for him, before we go to the State Trooper Headquarters."

This whole thing was getting messy. What would happen when Mr. Calhoun learned of the prank that was played on Teddy? What would happen when he found out the Troop lied? The Troop could be disbanded. All looked at each other through the corners of their eyes. The thought that this was Teddy's fault seemed to jump from one to the other.

After another mile, a figure swayed on the road's edge.

"Teddy, that has to be Teddy," Steve shouted, pointing needlessly.

The car slowed and, sure enough, it was Teddy.

"What are you doing?" Mr. Calhoun came to a stop and called out the window, fully relieved that a lost scout was found.

Teddy turned toward the Jeep. It was then that he saw Paul. The furrows on his face smoothed and the tear tracks melted into his skin.

"Where are you going?" Mr. Calhoun tried a second time.

Teddy took in the concerned faces.

All were worried that he would rat them out.

He scanned each Troop member's face then looked back again at Paul. Paul lowered himself and covered his face with his hands, wishing he was truly invisible.

Teddy's face was set and had a harsh look. "I got lost."

Mr. Calhoun thought for a moment then chose to believe it. "Okay, hop into the back."

"I'll ride in the back. Teddy, get in here." Steve opened the door and crammed himself in the back.

The boys felt gratitude toward Teddy, for five minutes at least. However, Teddy had worked up a good sweat running and walking. His body order permeated the entire interior.

"Wow! You smell worst than Gary!" Kenny said and rolled down a window.

Gary gave Kenny a deadly stare.

"Ugh!"

"Teddy do you know what soap is?"

"Pee yew."

"I'm going to gag again!"

Everyone joined in the tease.

Normalcy had returned in short order.

The Scout Troop lasted for another year. As the boys entered high school, interests diverged and each made other groups of friends.

Teddy became lost in the halls of high school. When two or more of the old Troop bumped into one another, the talk would eventually come around to that hunting trip and Teddy.

By the end of high school, no one knew what happened to him. Rumor was that he rode a scooter into Stirling Lake and drowned.

Gary stopped attending Scout meetings and dropped out of school. He too disappeared from the Troop.

Chapter 5

Like the sun moving out of cloud cover, the real solution showed itself. For years I had endured these events and more. Now I knew how to end it and it would begin with the Scout Troop! More memories fought to be released. I exhaled, expelling some of what I had hid for so long. I hugged the shoe-box. Everything was so clear now.

Relief was a warm blanket. I felt whole with clarity of thought and purpose. Warmth enveloped me. Outside the sun shone as if God himself were giving me directions. I slept through the afternoon. Tonight plans would be made.

ഇരുന

K.J. Richardson awoke to a hazy summer morning with a forecast of high temperatures, but things were good. He was rising in the law firm. Natural born superiority had led the way all his life. Kenny whistled as he dressed. His business meeting today could be the big event catapulting his career. Tonight, he would meet his girlfriend for dinner and, hopefully, would give her good news—no, make that great news. In the back of his mind, he wondered if his girlfriend was worthy of their relationship. He had had so many before that just didn't make the grade, but no time to worry about that now.

Summer days were never good in the City. K.J. walked slowly so he wouldn't sweat or wrinkle his suit in the eighty-degree afternoon. At the office, he redressed in a blue Alan David tailored suit with a light silk blue tie and loaded his eel skin valise with the proposal he was offering today. He wanted to appear crisp and professional. This business lunch at Hill Country could mean a partnership in the law firm of Daley, Ryan & Forthsmith. He didn't particularly enjoy barbecue, but understood that Kevin Jacobs of the nonprofit foundation, Children Are Our Future, did. The foundation wanted to go global and this could be an anchor client for the firm.

At noon on the corner of Sixth Avenue, K.J. entered into the smell of Texas.

Damn, now I'll have to dry clean my suit to get rid of this smoke, he thought as he looked around the dark, quarter-sawn oak paneled room. He had only talked with

Jacobs over the phone and had never met him. The agreed rendezvous was a table under a huge star relief at the end of the dining room. K.J. grabbed a folded napkin from an empty table to quickly wipe his face and hands then tossed it onto another empty table.

The ridiculously big star wasn't hard to find hanging on the wall at the end of the room.

Two tables under it were occupied by couples, one was empty, and at the fourth sat a balding middle-aged man in a motorized wheelchair wearing a white micro suede western jacket, twill light blue work shirt, and a black bolo. This caught K.J. by surprise. "He's a cripple!"

K.J. composed himself, put on his best lawyer smile, and approached the table. "Mr. Jacobs?"

"Yes." His right hand reached over his stomach. K.J. had to bend over to shake it. "And you are Mr. Richardson."

"Yes."

"Good, Good. Sit down. This is a great place to meet since I'm from Texas and live for barbecue beef brisket Texas style. I couldn't negotiate that big building you are in anyway—no handicap facilities."

K.J. sat opposite Jacobs. This wasn't going well. "We have repeatedly asked the landlord to do something about that," he lied and felt good at his quick reply.

"Well, son, that's why the foundation was created. People overlook or don't want to see impairments, especially children with disabilities. Adults get the lion's share of attention and funds and I mean the lion's share— all of it. Children of all ages get lost in the system. Why, some of them are even made fun of. I know. I was the butt of many a practical jokes when I was young. I wanted to fit in, so for a long time I tolerated it."

Nothing registered with K.J. He tried to look at the menu to find something that wouldn't drip and stain his suit.

"A 2010 survey by the U.S. Census Bureau reported 2.8 million school-aged children with disabilities. Globally, children have accounted for approximately twenty to thirty percent of all casualties from landmines, remnants of cluster munitions, and other explosive remains of war. UNICEF estimates that there are 150 million children with disabilities world-wide. The majority of these children live in developing countries that don't have rehabilitative heath care facilities. But enough of this for now. Let's order lunch. I recommend the barbecue beef brisket. It's the state dish of the Republic of Texas."

K.J. stared at the menu. It was clear that Jacobs wasn't going to order first. "I'll take your advice and have the chopped brisket sandwich." K.J opened his valise and took out a large spiral enclosed document and slid it across the table. "Perhaps you could read this as we eat."

"Excellence choice! I'm going to have the moist brisket with a side of Texas black-eyed caviar." Jacobs leaned forward and winked. "You know, in Exodus 12:9, it says 'Do not eat the meat raw or boiled in water, but roast it over a fire.'"

K.J. gave Jacobs his client smile.

The lunch went well. K.J. played with the sandwich, opening it then pushing the brisket around his plate to make it look like he was eating this crap. Jacobs ate in earnest, devouring everything. While he licked his fingers, he seemed satisfied with the accomplishments of Daley, Ryan & Forthsmith and the draft of expected legal situations, solutions, and legal needs for Children Are Our Future expansion.

Jacobs started to hand back the sauce stained document.

"No, no, take it with you."

"Okay, young man, I will."

K.J. paid the tab, shook hands, and left Jacobs at the table, happy to be far from the cripple. No matter, this would be huge. A meeting next week with the law firm's principles would seal the deal and his future.

Richardson walked into bright sunlight and started to cross Twenty-Sixth Street. Today was a good day.

He heard the red car before he saw it. Turning around, K.J. instantly realized it was too late to move to safety.

The car hit him midsection. K.J. was thrown twenty feet onto the side walk. His head hit first and cracked open like a watermelon falling off a market shelf. The last thing K.J. thought before his eyes glazed over and his brain emptied on the pavement was, *Why me*?

⌘⌘⌘

Steve, Paul, Peter, and Clancy stood in the back looking at the coffin where Kenny lay in the front. Large bouquets of flowers gave the room a sickly scent. The coolness of the viewing room accented the paleness of Kenny's features. He wore his blue Alan David suit with the light blue silk tie. The only good in that day was his blood and brains oozed into the gutter and never stained the suit.

"Well, the Troop is back together again," Steve half heartily joked.

"Kenny in spirit and Teddy absent. You guys know what ever happened to him? Did he really die in a motor-cycle accident?"

"No, Peter, I don't think he would pass the driver's test for a motorcycle. He just disappeared."

"Did they catch the driver who mowed down Ken-ny?" Paul whispered.

"No the car sped away and, like Teddy, disap-peared."

"That's a shame. Kenny was on his way up."

"Yeah, and a random accident brought him down."

"I don't think it was random. I heard the car actually was on the sidewalk when it hit him. In fact, observers saw the car move out of a parking spot up the street and speed up."

"What are you saying, Steve? That it was intentional?"

"Through my position with the newspaper, I was able to get in touch with the Tenth precinct and received the patrolman's report as well as his notes about the incident which included the eyewitness observations. Moreover, the car was found in an abandoned lot. It had been stolen in New Jersey."

"Any fingerprints or clues?"

"Unfortunately, none. No fingerprints or anything else. You know most police precincts in New York are understaffed and under budget. They don't have the sophisticated equipment you see on TV or the time to really investigate."

"How about street video cameras?" Paul whispered.

"One recorded the car and license plate, but not a clear view of the driver."

"So no motivation then," Paul concluded.

"I guess they investigated Kenny's clients and colleagues. Don't know the outcome or if a motivation was discovered"

The group became silent with thoughts about the unexpected death of a friend. The room buzzed with low voices like flies over carrion.

Mr. Calhoun was talking with Kenny's parents. His hair was completely gray now and he had a noticeable stoop. Lilies masked the scent of bourbon infused over the years in his now-wrinkled skin. A few high school classmates were present. Kenny's relatives wept in chairs near the coffin. A small coterie of black suits sat on the end rows for quick exits. What the Troop missed was a still figure standing in the far back corner with his hands folded along his worn belt buckle. A shabby sports coat extended beyond his wrists. His hair was partly combed. He was the only one in the room smiling. He stared not at the coffin, but at Steve, Paul, Peter, and Clancy.

All but this one sat down as the pastor approached the bier.

"Kenneth James Richardson was a Scout, a loving son, a rising lawyer, and a good man. He appreciated everyone and was involved in many charities. Jesus said, 'This is the will of my Father that everyone who sees the Son and believes in him may have eternal life, and I shall raise him up on the last day.'"

The man in the corner left after the pastor finished the second sentence.

The interment was at Holy Cross Cemetery, a small exclusive memorial park. Trees and rose bushes were carefully laid out in the green meadow. Kenny's grave was on the hillside overlooking all those who rested here.

Bodies as well as eyes shed water as the sun burned over the gravesite. Less than an hour later, it was over. Those invited drove to the repast.

The same cliques that formed at the wake gathered at

the Chimney Rock Inn, minus the lawyers. The restaurant was named after a tall column of rock on high land once shared by the Raritan and Manhattan Indians. The rock was a strategic location for the Raritans. Two chieftains from each tribe had met by the rock during a peace period and became friendly.

The Raritan chief eventually offered his daughter, Chinqueka, to the Manhattan chief, Capatamin, hoping to extend the peace interlude, but a sub-chief of the Raritans wanted Chinqueka for his own. One night as Capatamin and Chinqueka stood near the rock, looking into the valley and, perhaps, their future, the sub-chief rushed from concealment, cleaved Capatamin's head with his tomahawk, and pushed him over the cliff to the stream below. After days of bereavement, Chinqueka threw herself off the cliff. The sub-chief lived on with three wives.

So in a restaurant named for a murder scene, the Troop continued the discussion about the cause of Kenny's death.

"Why would anyone want to kill Kenny?"

"We don't know," Steve answered Peter's question. "But something is suspicious."

Clancy gobbled up the slow smoked ribs not paying attention to ongoing conversation. "This food is really good."

"Well, I think our lives must be dull to think Kenny might have been murdered."

"Perhaps, you're right Paul. There's no reason, but

accidents do happen. God can't watch us all."

Mr. Calhoun appeared behind his former Troop. "How's everything going?"

Heads turned with a listlessness mumbling.

"You know things happen. Some that can't be explained."

"Some of us think he was murdered," Paul whispered.

"Really? What makes you think that?"

"Steve says that the car was waiting for Kenny."

"Nonsense. It was an accident that perhaps appeared to be more. People always read into things that are not there. Let's just concentrate on Kenny and remember him in a better light. Don't think any more than that." Mr. Calhoun patted each on the shoulder, once again taking the role as Troop Leader as he gave each one an odd stare as if he was judging something before he moved on.

"I guess he's right."

"You know, this is the first time we got together in a long while. We need to plan another gathering on better terms. What do you say?" Steve asked the others. He wanted to show the Troop that conspiracies were a part of everyday life.

All nodded.

After an hour, the repast ended and the Troop went to their homes and family, agreeing to meet in a month.

⊱⊰⊱

Satisfaction. No more than that. Pleasure! Yes, pleasure. The hard crunching impact and the surprised look on Kenny's face. Was it from the hit or did he recognize me? I couldn't help smiling and started rocking in place. That was the most enjoyment I'd had in a long time. It was perfect planning—something I hadn't been able to do before. I just wished I had time to see him sprawled on the sidewalk. I had hoped to run over him as well. I had been thinking about this for a long time. It was good to be free from self-enforced restraint.

Now for the next.

Chapter 6

The remaining Troop met on a Saturday afternoon at the Stirling House Diner on Valley Road. A middle-aged waitress asked for their order. She wore black gloves and seemed annoyed with her job. "What do you want?"

Clancy wasn't finished reading the menu. "We need a little more time."

"Take your time. I'm here all day." The waitress left without asking about beverages.

Paul looked at the retreating figure. "Wow, she wasn't polite. It's a shame the way some people treat each other."

"All right, did everyone do their homework?" Steve asked the group.

"I still agree with Mr. Calhoun. Kenny was an accident. Why are we still obsessed with it?" Paul questioned.

"Because of the circumstances. There may be a pattern here we don't see. Don't you see? All right, let's look at who died since high school," Steve began.

"Your brother come up with anything regarding Kenny?" Peter asked.

"We will get to that later. Let's just see if anyone in our class died suspiciously. Rob Walsh. He died in Vietnam, right?"

"Well, not in Vietnam, but afterward. He died of Agent Orange. Dioxin gave him cancer." Clancy checked the notes he had brought along with the Watchung Hills Regional High School yearbook for 1965. "Nothing suspicious. Then there's Mark Albani. He died of head injuries from football while at Syracuse. Nothing suspicious here either."

"Anybody else?"

"Well, I searched the obituaries and found Rich Slager. He was suffocated with a pillow by his roommate at Penn State."

"Who was the roommate?"

"Someone from Arkansas."

"So there is nothing to connect these with Kenny. Nothing!" Paul stated.

"Not that we know," replied Steve.

"How about those who just are missing?" Clancy asked.

"There were a lot 'part-timers' who came and went."

"Like who?"

"Well, there's Gary Wilton. He was a weird one. Anyone know what happened to him?"

Before an answer could be given, the waitress came back and demanded an order.

The order for simple burgers was given for all, except Clancy who ordered a Roast Sirloin of Beef and Swiss Triple Decker sandwich with sides of curly fries, onion rings, and potato salad. Steve ordered a shot of Jack Daniels.

"Jesus, Steve, booze this early?"

"Just something to get along, Peter."

After the meal and while Clancy ate his favorite desert, vanilla fudge sundae, the conversation continued.

"Okay, any more news from your brother?" Paul asked again.

"No, the case is cold now. It's officially a hit-and-run—an accident."

"Then why are we here?"

"Because I don't believe it. I don't think the cops are working that hard. Nothing is random."

"But Kenny was jaywalking. It was his fault."

"I don't know. There's something about this. Something we are missing." Steve urged the others, "You just have to look."

"Since we are reviewing out past associates' whereabouts, where did Teddy go?"

"Didn't he ride a scooter into Stirling Lake and drown?"

"That was a rumor. I don't remember a funeral."

"His family probably couldn't afford it and buried him in the backyard."

"That's not funny, Peter."

"So," Paul began to sum up the afternoon, "We had a fairly decent lunch and didn't come up with a 'conspiracy.'" He had placed air quotes around "conspiracy."

Steve was annoyed at the gesture. "Fine, fine, let's go."

Perhaps they would see later.

⁊ↄ⁊ↄ

Clancy walked up the creaky back stairs to his older brother's room, which had once been servants' quarters, stopping once to catch his breath. How many times had he done this since his parents passed away? He didn't want to remember. His brother, Gordon, was "displaced," as his parents named his condition. To Clancy, he was either retarded or crazy. Gordon was allowed to roam the house when his parents were alive so Clancy hadn't dared to invite over any friends in his youth—especially the Troop because of how they treated Teddy. Clancy's dislike of the Troop's attitude toward the disadvantaged had grown as his family burden did even after all these years, but they were the few friends he had left. Clancy wasn't surprised about Steve's conspiracy theories. Everything in this world had been against Steve through no fault of his own other than his imagination.

Now, with few friends and less interest in entertaining, taking care of Gordon was more than enough for Clancy.

The money his parents willed to him stipulated personal care for Gordon—for this secret had to remain within the family. His resentment of his displaced brother also grew. Clancy had removed Gordon from a front bedroom, not realizing what this meant psychologically.

Clancy had to sacrifice his senior year at Princeton and much of everything else. This house on Long Hill Road became more of prison every day.

Clancy opened the white bedroom door. "Gordon, you awake? It's time."

From under quilted covers a blond disheveled head broke through. "What?"

"It's time for breakfast."

"What time is it?"

"Time for breakfast, Gordie. Get up."

Unlike Clancy, Gordon was lean, almost to an emaciated state. Clancy helped dress him and escorted him to the kitchen. The damn will demanded that Gordon remain in the house—didn't specify where—and that Clancy care for him as his parents had. This meant dressing him and food served in the dining room not in the bedroom. At least Gordon could use the bathroom by himself.

Holding on to his arm, Clancy escorted Gordon down the steps, ignoring urges to push him on the steep narrow staircase.

Bacon and eggs, with the eggs fried in the bacon fat, and a glass of orange juice were placed in front of Gordon. Three times a day Clancy wondered what he would do if Gordon couldn't feed himself. For now, he was content that Gordon ate, no matter how much.

Food was delivered by the ShopRite market in Stirling. All Clancy had to do was call in the order. An account had been established. The only irritating part was that the deliveryman seemed to change frequently and the ice cream was almost always melting.

Gordon finished eating and playing with his breakfast.

Clancy took his hand and led him to the den, turned on the television, pointed to the corner shelves stacked with toys and puzzles, and left the room.

That should hold him till lunch, Clancy thought hopefully. Sara, the caretaker was due around one p.m. and would stay till bedtime at nine.

At 12:30, the doorbell rang. Without Sara, Clancy trudged to the front of the house to find out who was there. A new delivery man, wearing a gray hoodie that covered most of his face, stood with a dolly loaded with paper grocery bags waiting for instructions.

This was a day early for delivery and Sara usually took care of this. Clancy was slightly confused and annoyed that this driver didn't use the delivery entrance in back.

"In here, mind the carpet. Follow me." Clancy led him to the kitchen.

The delivery man placed all the grocery bags on the kitchen table. His head was tilted down as he stood still.

Clancy didn't know if he was expecting a tip. As he dug in his pocket for his wallet, the man left. Clancy followed behind to the door. "Thank you," he said to the retreating figure.

Back in the kitchen, Clancy noticed one of the bags was leaking. Sure enough it was the ice cream container. He placed it in the sink and brought two bags of groceries to the pantry and the perishable bags of vegetables and fruit to the refrigerator. He seemed to remember the groceries usually came in boxes and now there were items he never encountered before. Perhaps Sara had ordered these. Intent on placing each known item in its designated spot, he didn't notice that Gordon had wandered into the kitchen.

Going for another bag, he saw Gordon by the sink. "What are you doing?"

Gordon was sticking his hand in the ice cream and licking each finger. "I like vanilla, too!"

"You don't eat with your fingers!" Clancy admonished him. He washed Gordon's hand and led him back into the den. Sara couldn't come soon enough.

Back in the kitchen, Clancy was tempted to eat the

ice cream, but Gordon's finger molds quickly erased that thought. He washed out the container and threw it in the kitchen waste basket under the sink.

Sara finally showed and prepared lunch for Gordon.

Clancy was free for the rest of the day. He walked slowly to the back white barn. A red barn was for farmers. Clancy unlocked the tall wooden doors and stepped in front of a canvas-covered object. He carefully removed the cover, and a bright blue 1930 Model L Lincoln automobile was revealed. The Model L had a 383.8 cubic-inch flathead V8 engine with aluminum pistons for ninety horsepower. It had dual folding windshields and could seat seven. It was magnificent: all original parts. The car had been in the family for generations.

Clancy opened a cabinet and took out polish compound and a microfiber cloth. Slowly, he covered the entire car and then wiped the wax off. Time was irrelevant during these rituals.

Finished, he caressed the left fender, moved his hand over the white-walled spare tire attached to the side, and opened the door. Behind the steering wheel, he recalled the times the family went to New York City and Boston for the theater and other events. Gordon was almost normal then. They were great times, but then Gordon had turned and the family became isolated with their shame. The car was placed in the barn and only started up occasionally to insure running condition.

What would the Troop say if they had known of this

beautiful car while attempting to find one to smash. They were an ignorant bunch, after all.

In the mist of these thoughts, he didn't hear Sara yelling his name. When she came running, he finally was brought to reality.

"Mr. Dickerson, Mr. Dickerson! Something is wrong with Gordon!"

"What?"

"His nose and gums are bleeding. He had diarrhea."

"Crap!" Clancy followed behind Sara into the house.

His asthma erupted in the sprint toward the house. Clancy frantically searched his pockets for his inhaler. Finding it, he slumped to the un-mowed turf and breathed in the aerosol heavily, hoping he didn't have grass stains on his trousers.

Sara realized Clancy wasn't near as she reached the house. Seeing him on the lawn, she froze for a moment, trying to decide who to help. Then as Clancy was getting up, she went to Gordon. He was on his stomach on the den floor, moaning and rocking side-to-side. His pants were soiled and he held a towel Sara had given him to his face. Sara removed the towel and gave him a fresh one.

Clancy entered the den wheezing and his face redder than usual.

"I think he needs to go to the hospital," she said.

"Did you call 911?" Clancy asked.

"No, I was waiting for you to determine how bad he is."

"Okay, I'll call." Clancy didn't want to have Gordon in his car with diarrhea.

The Millington First Aid Squad arrived within ten minutes and rushed him to Morristown Memorial. Clancy declined to ride in the ambulance because of the step up and cramped quarters. There was nothing he could do, anyway.

Clancy followed in his Cadillac CTS Sedan, comfortable, but not as elegant as the Model L. He stopped at a McDonalds for light midday meal and went inside. It was lunch time, after all, and he was hungry.

After a meal of a Premium Grilled Chicken Classic—only 350 calories, medium French fries—only 380 calories, McCafe Nonfat Latte—only 130 calories, and a hot fudge vanilla sundae—only 510 calories, Clancy wiped his mouth and resumed his trip to the hospital.

After looking for a convenient parking space for several minutes, Clancy finally found one near the emergency entrance.

Upon inquiring about his brother, Clancy was instructed to go to the admitting desk. Gordon hadn't been looked after because the hospital did not have proper identification or medical insurance information. The seriousness of Gordon's condition did not seem to require immediate triage. In fact, Gordon was sitting on a faded green plastic chair in his own feces in the waiting room.

Clancy sat two chairs away from him. "It will be all right, Gordie. Don't worry."

A nurse finally came to escort Gordon to a treatment room. An emergency medicine physician began an examination. Blood work was ordered and a call went to the Dickerson family physician.

Gordon was admitted for further tests. Clancy went home.

The next day Clancy received a call.

"Gordon appears to have ingested rat poison."

"What? We certainly do not have rats."

"This poison probably is homemade poison containing gypsum, commonly called Plaster of Paris. Did you make any?"

"I told you, we do not have a rodent problem."

"Well, we will need to notify the police about this."

"What? Why?"

"Well, it is suspicious. You are his guardian and came here almost an hour after the ambulance arrived. The poison is home made."

"You are intimating that I wanted to kill my brother?"

"I am doing my duty, sir, not implying any judgment."

Clancy hung up, stunned at the development. Sure, once in a while he would day dream about life without Gordie, but never took steps to accomplish it. He picked up the phone to call his lawyer before the police arrived.

∽✦∽

"So I am now in agreement with Steve that there might be conspiracy." Clancy opened the Saturday lunch conversation at the Pizza Mill on Long Hill Road. They had enough of the waitress at the Stirling House Diner.

Steve leaned in to hear every word. "So what exactly happened?"

"You never met my brother, Gordon. He digested some rat poison. The authorities think I may be involved since the poison was home made. They make the premise that I wanted him out of the way for complete control over the inheritance. But the grocery delivery was early and there were things I never ordered before. Sara claimed she wasn't involved and didn't know anything about the order. I called the market and they claim there was never an order called in. And get this—the rat poison was in the ice cream that Gordon started to eat. There were still some traces in the container I threw away. If he ate more, he might be dead. So I saved his life!"

"You have a brother?"

"I just told you that."

"Who is Sara?"

"She's a part time maid." Clancy was afraid he was giving too much information.

"You have a maid? Wow!"

"I didn't recognize the delivery man and he had the groceries in paper bags, not boxes like usual. So on the heels of Kenny's death, this seems to be related. I think the ice cream was meant for me!"

"Yes, yes," Steve started to get into it. "Two of our Troop members attacked within months."

"I don't know if we can go that far." Paul shook his head. "You see a conspiracy in almost everything. Perhaps it was not the Troop, but anyone who had a 'son' at the end of a sir name. You see what I mean?"

"Did the delivery man have a ShopRite truck?"

"No, Steve. The deliveries are in private cars. These guys are temporary."

"Did you notice the car then?"

"No, I was too surprised by the delivery. I don't do those things."

"Okay. Why would anyone want to kill you, kill us?"

"You're jumping the gun again, Steve. We don't know if anyone is out to get 'us.'" Paul tried again to bring reason to the table. "Is Shoprite checking with the dairy that produced the ice cream?"

"Yes, they are."

"So perhaps they will find rats at the manufacturing plant."

A sixteen-inch pizza was brought to the small round table in the corner near a soda machine. Clancy searched for the larger cut. All were lost in thoughts as they ate the Neapolitan pie.

After the pizza plate was removed, the conversion began again.

"If you think you were a definite target, Clancy, are you going to get some sort of security?" Peter asked.

"No, no security."

"Why? You can afford it."

Clancy didn't want the family secret to be spread about even more. "I don't think it is necessary. Maybe, just maybe, I am wrong in seeing this as a conspiracy."

"No, man. Don't back off now. There is something to all this." Steve didn't want an ally to retreat.

"I think now it might be rat poison from the plant. ShopRite has recalled all brand ice cream regardless of the flavor. So they must suspect something."

"They have to do that to protect themselves. It isn't a judgment. It's corporate self-preservation."

"Let it rest, Steve."

The Troop departed, divided once again.

ℰℑℰℑ

Failure! That fat tub still lived! He hit the sides of his head in frustration. Clancy didn't even know who was responsible—the only good thing about this unsuccessful attempt. He might have been too clever this time. The physical approach was so much more satisfying anyway.

It would be different for the next time. So much delightful planning to do.

Chapter 7

Two months had passed since the event. Gordie was back to "normal." No further investigation by the police was forthcoming. ShopRite hadn't found obvious evidence for rat poison in the dairy plant. Clancy ignored calls from Steve.

The incident was slowly fading from his consciousness as he became obsessed with getting the Model L back on the road. Registration and insurance were nuisance paper work. Inspecting the old tires for stability, making sure the gas tank didn't contain degraded gas, checking the engine for corroded and non-working parts, examining the electrical system, and assessing the brakes were only a few items on his list of major things to do.

For many of these, he needed outside assistance,

which he was reluctant to bring to the house.

Tim Hardy owned a two-bay repair and gas station opposite the Millington Gypsum facility. Clancy always gassed up his Cadillac here and went for bi-annual state mandated inspections. While he didn't know Tim that well, he was the nearest mechanic and always treated Clancy with respect.

Clancy ventured outside his house for the first time in weeks, not that he had been afraid. He was just occupied with the Model L and had little social life apart from the occasional meetings of old Troop members.

Tim emerged from the garage office and greeted Clancy. Clancy explained his project of getting the Model L back on the road and the need for safety.

Tim told Clancy that he couldn't diagnose the automobile at its location. The car needed to be in a bay where he could lift it, where his tools and diagnostic equipment were. This was just the situation Clancy had hoped for. The next week Tim would come with his flatbed tow truck.

Clancy was relieved that Tim only needed to come to the house once. He drove back home in a good mood, unaware of the green car that had been parked in the same spot off Long Hill road near his house for the last two weeks.

On schedule, Tim arrived and, under Clancy's unneeded supervision, loaded the 1930 Lincoln. Tim was in awe. The Model L was in pristine condition. She was a beauty. Anyone would die to have it. Clancy followed the tow truck to the station. The automobile was carefully unloaded and pushed into a bay.

"I'll take it from here," Tim advised Clancy, hoping he wouldn't hang around. "A full inspection will take a couple of days."

Clancy reluctantly left and slowly walked over to the Millington Station Cafe which was the original station house situated near the Gladstone Branch of the Morris and Essex train tracks. A spur ran into the gypsum plant. The station was built in 1901 from gray stone blocks. Bright white trim framed the building. In 1984, it was entered into the National Register of Historic Places as part of the New Jersey Transit Thematic Nomination of Operating Passenger Railroad Stations. Because of this historic designation, the station was not accessible under the American with Disabilities Act. Clancy cursed silently as he stepped up on the high side platform to enter the building.

The cafe was nearly empty since it was between train schedules. Despite the two bagels and egg breakfast he had in the last hour, Clancy ordered a Taylor ham, egg, and cheese sandwich; a bagel with cream cheese; a side of Greek salad; and—always concerned for his health—a diet Coke. Unfortunately, the cafe didn't provide dessert since its patrons were mostly commuters and didn't have the time for treats.

As he left the building eating the third bagel of the

day, a figure quickly approached from behind, twisted Clancy's left arm behind his back, and in a gruff voice urged him to be quiet and continued walking down the vacant asphalt platform.

Clancy began to struggle and to call out. A piece of black wide electrical tape with a hole was rapidly placed over his mouth. A push to his back hurried Clancy along.

In a short time, the two moved into the woods behind the cafe toward the Millington Gorge. With a closed mouth and the exertion of walking faster than usual, Clancy's asthma began to attack him. He stumbled through the thick brush, gasping for air through his nose and fell. His assailant put on surgical gloves and assisted him up. He continued to push Clancy forward. At the edge of the gorge, Clancy was turned around.

A pint bottle of Jack Daniels was placed into his mouth through the hole in the tape.

Clancy heaved and gagged, his eyes watered and closed from the raw pain in his throat. Lunch gurgled up, filled his mouth, and poured out the tape hole. When he finished retching, the bottle was again roughly shoved in and emptied. More choking before he was able to look at his mugger through tears. The tape was ripped off and the bottle placed in Clancy's hand, the neck wiped clean and then thrown into the weeds.

"*You*!" Clancy managed to utter between raw coughs and spasms. He couldn't believe who he was facing. "*Why*?"

The response was a strong push that propelled Clancy down the hill. He slid on the leaves and through small brush, rolling uncontrollably.

His head hit a hickory tree but it didn't stop gravity from moving him onward. A birch cracked his ribs and ended the roll. Clancy lay moaning, but not for long. The attacker moved Clancy with some difficulty and kicked his stomach to continue the slide down. Clancy bounced off a dogwood and landed on the bank of the Passaic River, the left half of him in water.

The figure stood over the body. Clancy's eyes were dull. He was nearly unconscious.

"Wake up you fat pig!"

A slap to his face produced no results. The assailant turned Clancy's head into the brown polluted river, holding it down with his boot.

After a good amount of bubbles and no bodily movement, Clancy was propelled into the river. The body floated away to the Great Falls in Paterson.

❧❧❧

The remaining Troop sat at the bar of the Stirling Hotel after Clancy's funeral and repast. Steve ordered a Jack Daniels. Peter and Paul had ginger ales. A gloom had settled over them.

Steve started the conversation. "I'm surprised at the small attendance. I thought there would be more."

"I don't think he had a lot of friends," Peter said. "Mr. Calhoun was there. We have seen him more times these last months than over the last fifteen years. It's a shame something bad has to bring people together."

"They said Clancy was drunk and wandered into the gorge," Paul commented. "He had a blood alcohol concentration of 0.09 percent. They found the bottle."

"But Clancy didn't drink," Peter said. "And that is just over the legal limit."

"This is part of the conspiracy I've been trying to tell you about," Steve parried. "Someone is hiding something. Someone is out to get us!"

"Crap, Steve," Peter retorted. "I'm tired of that. Personally I think he was food drunk."

"Food drunk?"

"Yes, Steve. He probably was brewing booze in his stomach due to a buildup of Saccharomyces cerevisiae— common yeast in his gut. He ate like a pig and when he ate starch-heavy foods, including bagels, pasta, and soda, and he ate quite a lot, the yeast in his belly fermented the sugars into ethanol. Food drunkenness is a physiological state after consuming large amounts of food."

"Then how come the autopsy didn't find this?"

"It's a rare buildup. A man in Texas had the same thing. It was in the *International Journal of Clinical Medicine*. Besides, postmortem blood alcohol concentrations are less reliable and stable than those obtained from the living."

"Just because you're a doctor and can quote some obscure article doesn't make it any less probable than someone or some persons killing Clancy. I mean, look what happened recently to him."

"Well, what evidence do you have to support your theory?"

"He had grease stains on the back of his shirt. Clancy was always fastidious about his clothes."

"He was at a garage."

"Sure, but I can't imagine him going into the bays or anywhere near anything dirty."

"So someone with greasy hands was involved."

"Exactly. Someone who works around cars."

"Like Tim Hardy."

"Possibly."

"And what would be his motive?"

"The Model L. Maybe he thought it would be forgotten after Clancy was gone."

"So why would Tim kill Kenny? He probably didn't even know him."

Steve shook his head. "I don't know why. I'll have to think about it."

"Well, think all you want. It is highly unlikely that two of our friends would die in such a short period of time. But it is more unlikely that one particular person caused it."

"What would you think if it happened again?"

"Don't be ridiculous, Steve."

 espeso

Who did this? He'd wanted to dispatch that tub of lard. He failed once. Now he would never experience the thrill of taking Clancy's life. It seemed his God-given powers had diminished. He felt deprived and insulted. He must find out who before the police did, if they indeed did.

He must take this poacher's life in place of Dickerson's. This person would not dilute his mission!

Chapter 8

Mr. Calhoun sat in the 1950 cottage's dimly lit living room, looking at old photos fixed to the flowered wall. When built, the cottage could have been featured in a Thomas Kinkade painting. Now it needed paint and more attention to the landscape.

His wife had died long ago and, now a retired certified public accountant, Mr. Calhoun felt very lonely. Looking back, his only accomplishments had been passing the Uniform Certified Public Accountant Examination and being a Scout Master.

No one had ever called him by his given name, Jack. He had always been Mr. Calhoun. Maybe that was a sign of respect, but it became all too cold over the years.

No work to go to, no scout meetings, it seemed that

his only entertainment now was funerals. Jack looked at the wall full of photos of the Troop—smiling faces and group activities. Snapshots of Kenny and Clancy had been removed.

Jack poured another shot of Jack Daniels. The sad truth, though, was that he was never a good Scout Master. The Troop were never good Scouts and that was his fault. They were cruel and misbehaving at times, times he should have been there. But the Troop added a meaning to his life then, so he could forgive. Now, thinking back, it was a mistake not to take seriously the boys' attitude about scouting and it was a major blemish to his rather monotonous life. Jack had routines to fill his last days:

Usually cleaning the house of unused or unwanted items made him feel positive about his new existence. Walking to the Millington Station Cafe for a morning cup of coffee gave him a purpose to wake up.

Weekly shopping at the ShopRite in Stirling gave him sustenance.

Driving his green 1982 Ford Fairmont in parts of New Jersey he hadn't been before gave him escape.

Driving to familiar locations gave Jack reasons to review his past and consider his future.

As the sun set, he looked at the photo wall and where the missing photos had been. Things were becoming correct.

∽⌒∽⌒

Steve walked to the front door of Peter and Paul's manicured colonial house.

It had taken him awhile to comprehend their situation after he learned they were a couple years ago. He had suspected something in the scouting days, but was too unknowing to understand.

Paul let him in. Antiques proliferated the house. Old wood and brass polish suffocated the environment.

"Anything new to show?" Steve asked to be polite.

"Oh, yes!" Paul excitedly led Steve to a bedroom where he pointed to a polished oak dresser with three drawers and a back shelf. It had an adjustable mirror and fancy wood carvings.

Steve was uncomfortable in the bedroom, but needed to say something. "Nice. How old is it?"

"It was made circa 1800. Hand carved. It's in great condition."

"That is nice." Steve couldn't keep up the conversation. "Is Peter around?"

"Yes, come to the kitchen."

The kitchen was large with antique molds and kitchen utensils carefully placed on the walls.

Peter was seated at a wood farmhouse table, warming his hands around a cup of oolong tea. "Ah, Steve, come with another conspiracy?"

Steve ignored his remark. "No, I don't think it is a conspiracy anymore, but I am certain someone or some bodies are after us. I wondered if you knew what happened to Teddy Nestor–he didn't drown, that was only a rumor. How about Gary Wilton? I'm going to his house after here. I thought you might be able to fill me in before I go."

"Why?"

"Well, they were a part of our Troop. I just wanted to know if they're still alive."

"Gary lived just up the street from you. You haven't seen him or bumped into him all this time?"

"No, I've been busy."

"Great excuse."

"Well, I'm going now. I want to find out what he has been doing."

"Doing? You think either of them has been threatened? Are you still stuck with the conspiracy theory! You better sit down and have some tea." Peter looked at Paul who went to the cupboard and place a teacup and saucer in front of Steve.

"No, I just told you it is not a conspiracy. It's more sinister than that. The Troop is being hunted down."

"Wow! This is even worse. I think you need help, pal. Anyway, Steve, you're an editor for *Echoes-Sentinel*. Can't you find them? And why haven't you written about this theory of yours?"

"Well, I thought I'd start here, in case you had any information. I'm doing ground work and, as a matter of fact, I did bring this up to the managing editor, but because I didn't have hard evidence, he turned it down."

"You know, we don't know anything about those boys. We would never keep in contact with those two."

Steve took a polite sip of tea. "Really?"

"Of course. Do you remember them?"

"Sure, I do."

"To be frank, they are not in our social circle. Don't forget you don't know about their whereabouts either. Don't waste your time. Even your managing editor doesn't believe you."

"I see. Okay, I'll be going."

"Steve, for your own sake, get rid of this thought pattern. You'll be suspecting us next." Peter and Paul shot glances at each other, either out of amusement or concern.

Steve started his way to the front door. "No, I don't think you have the balls to kill someone."

Paul gave Steve a hard look with a slight smile. "Deuteronomy 32:35, 'To me belongeth vengeance, and recompense; their foot shall slide in due time: for the day of their calamity is at hand, and the things that shall come upon them make haste.'"

Outside, Steve wondered why he came here and what Paul meant. Maybe he did think there was a determined killer and didn't want Peter to hear. Steve's mood lightened at the thought. And, of course, they wouldn't keep in touch with those two. None of the Scouts had. Well, down to pavement pounding, direct research: real reporter work! Steve would visit Gary's old house and inquire where he was. Peter and Paul would soon see the dangers that lurked about, thought Steve.

Steve pulled into the rock and dirt driveway of Gary's decaying ranch house.

White washed tire rims, now showing rust, still lined the house perimeter. Vestiges of plants were piled in brown clumps inside the rims. Dandelions were still abundant throughout the unkempt front yard. The lawn hid many more rusting car parts. Steve wondered if the floors were still polished dirt. Surely town ordinance wouldn't allow that now.

The junkyard behind the house looked smaller and unused.

Steve knocked on the door, waited, and then knocked again. No answer. Just as he turned away, the door opened. Gary Wilton Junior stood in the entrance. Scattered behind him were opened and sealed boxes on a concrete floor. His facial features were similar to his father's. He was taller and had a powerful build.

"What do you want?"

Steve looked at the young Gary. "I guess I'm looking for your father."

"He left weeks ago."

"Is he still around here?"

"Why do you want to know?"

"I just want to renew an old friendship."

"Who are you, anyway?"

"Steve Mazur. Your father was in our Scout Troop."

"Oh yeah, yeah. He hated you and the Troop. Did you know that?"

"Hated us?"

"Of course. You treated him like shit!"

"We did?"

"Damn straight you did."

"I was unaware."

"Bull shit, you were."

"I was! Are you moving?"

"Organizing my father's stuff that he left, not that it's any of your business. Now get off my property."

"Do you know where he is?"

"No. He's around here somewhere. He doesn't contact me. And I wouldn't look for him if I was you. He's gone a little crazy."

"Crazy?"

"Don't find out how crazy. Now get out of here."

Steve attempted to inquire further, but the slam of the door solidified the end of the conversation.

ஐஇஐ

Giovanni Baglio stared at the gray bubbly water in the wash tub. He plunged his right arm in and searched for any dishes or glasses left at the bottom. His thoughts weren't on cleaning tableware though. They were about an incident a while back—one that remained in the forefront of his conscious now. As he brought clean beer glasses to the bar that day, he had spotted Steve Mazur, Paul Moody, and Peter Weber sitting at the far end of the Stirling HotelBar talking.

He knew what they were talking about: Richardson's and Dickerson's deaths. He had to smile. Good riddance to bad rubbish. He had tried to join Troop 186, but couldn't stand the way he was treated. His name was Giovanni, not wop, dego, guinea, or Guido. They treated him like something less than human, even if they couched it in humor. He didn't stay in the Troop for long and always remained outside the cliques in school. He knew he was a loner but this inconspicuously served him well.

The trio didn't even recognize him that day. Involuntarily, he rubbed the burn scar on his cheek.

They all went to college. He didn't have the smarts or the support to go. So he washed dishes for all these years. The success of the Troop and his situation were constant threads in his life. The deaths of the two were a bright light for his dull and unfulfilling existence.

He would see more of the "boys" now. You could count on that. Giovanni pulled the plug from the tub and watched all the dirty water drain away just like his life.

∽∾∽∾

Steve drove his Buick to Teddy's house. He tried to remember the times his mother drove Teddy home. As he turned onto Essex Street, he searched for the white wood-framed house with peeling paint he remembered. These were factory houses: built for knitting machines then turned into residential housing when the knitting market tumbled so long ago. The problem was that each house had the same architecture and all were white to some degree.

He finally settled on the worst-looking house on the silent block. The lawn was ragged. The paint on the house was almost completely stripped away, and the windows needed washing so much that it probably was a constant gray inside. A dirty weathered tarp covered a motorcycle parked forever on the crumbling paved side driveway. A graying flat tire poked from under the cover. Seeds, unfortunately dropped by birds or the wind, became trapped in the broken macadam and struggled for life. Despair veiled everything, even on a bright day.

Steve knocked on the front door, not expecting to find Teddy home. The window curtain next to the door moved slightly. Steve stepped back, a little startled. He waited a minute longer. The neighborhood was deserted. The curtain had been the only sign of life. Steve felt alone and vulnerable on this ghost street and began to second guess this visit as he waited for the door to be opened.

As he thought of knocking again, or fleeing, the door opened. Teddy stood looking at him.

He nearly looked the same. His features were more rounded and his hair was roughly combed. Teddy's face wasn't flushed, but still unnaturally pale. He stood motionless. He had grown and slightly towered over Steve. He seemed to embody more self-esteem.

"Teddy!" was all Steve could blurt out.

"Yes, Steve. I'm surprised to see you here."

Teddy didn't invite Steve in. He leaned on the door-frame with folded arms blocking the entrance.

"Have you heard of Kenny's and Clancy's death?"

"Yes, what of it?"

"Well, what do you make of it?"

"What do you mean?"

"Two members of our Troop have died in a relatively short time."

"So?"

"Don't you think this is suspicious?"

"Why would I?"

Struggling to continue the conversation with Teddy, Steve switched topics. "We thought you had drowned in a motorcycle accident."

"I haven't and don't drive a motorcycle anymore."

Steve glanced down the driveway and saw a green 1974 green Ford Galaxie partial hidden behind the house. "That yours?"

"Yes it is. I tamed it."

Steve didn't understand the reply. "Listen, can I come in to discuss this?"

"No. There is nothing to discuss. You always had an attitude and this is the first time you have visited since high school. Now you come with death on your lips."

Slightly unnerved by Teddy's sharp and articulate tongue, Steve answered lamely, "I've been busy." He became aware that it was the second time this day he had used the phrase.

"Not busy enough to get together with other Troop members."

"Well, we were talking about the deaths. You know, it wasn't by random that they met their end."

"Probably."

"You mean you suspect something too?"

"I'm not ruling out possibilities."

"We do need to talk then."

"I don't think so, Steve. We haven't talked in all this years and I've lived here all this time."

"Yeah, well, we need to talk now."

"Why would I care about the Troop now?"

"What?"

"You guys treated me like shit, like some scruffy pet."

"No, we didn't. It was fun times, joking, poking at each other. We were good kids."

"If you think so, you're fooling yourself. In Judges 15:7, 'Samson said to them, "Since you've acted like this, I won't stop until I get my revenge on you,"' Teddy forcefully intoned as he stared directly at Steve.

Steve ignored the stare, happy to have someone believe in him. "Ah, so you do believe that these deaths weren't accidents?"

But Teddy closed the door, leaving Steve on the porch to consider what exactly happened and why Teddy mentioned revenge. He thought of knocking again, but didn't since Teddy had never been right. This showed he was still the same. No one would believe Teddy.

Clouds started to cover the sun. It seemed the gray inside had leaked out when Teddy had opened the door. Steve began to wonder what he was doing in his supposed research.

But he had one last stop in his ground research. Driving past the Millington Station Cafe and Tim Hardy's repair shop where the garage bay doors were closed, he found Mr. Calhoun's cottage and was hopeful that he was home.

Mr. Calhoun had a door buzzer. Steve gazed at it. No more knocking. Maybe this was a sign. His index finger pressed the button. An irritating ring could be heard inside.

Steve again waited by the door as he had done all day. He heard rustling like old clothes being tossed in a dryer. The door opened. Mr. Calhoun seemed happy that a visitor came calling and even more so that it was a familiar face.

"Steve! Welcome. Come in."

Mr. Calhoun guided Steve past the living room into the dining room. The house seemed small—no, rather cramped with family histories, all trapped wanting to get out. Photos from generations back lined the walls. An

Edwardian mahogany serving table and an English walnut breakfront buffet sideboard were all Steve could name, and only this thanks to the influence of Paul. Steve felt a little confined with such massive furniture in a small room.

"Sit down, my boy." Mr. Calhoun pointed to the chair opposite him as he sat down. "What a pleasant surprise."

"Can we move to another room?"

Mr. Calhoun dismissed Steve's request. "This is fine. Sit down, my boy."

Steve sat at the barley twist dining room table.

"How have you been doing, Mr. Calhoun?"

"Fine, fine, but now that you are a man, please call me Jack."

"Okay, Jack. I came here to inquire if you have any thoughts about the recent deaths."

"Thoughts? Well, I'm so sorry and sad about Kenny and Clancy."

"We all are, but what I mean is, do you think there was anything behind this?"

"What do you mean, my boy?"

"Well, it seems unusual that Kenny and Clancy would both die by accidents in such a short period of time."

Jack leaned back. "Things happen, some for a reason, some without."

"I think there is a reason."

"Really?"

"Yes. And I'm worried that there will be another 'accident.'"

"Don't worry. It will get you nothing but fear and grief."

"Frankly, I'm worried about myself."

"I don't think you have anything to be afraid of, for now."

"For now?"

"We all die, my boy."

"But don't you think something is suspicious?"

"Steve, you can make anything suspicious. Let me tell you a story. When I was young, I had a best friend, Freddie. We would do everything together. One day we went to the Gorge. Freddie was determined to paint his name on the trestle. If we were smart, we would have picked up a train schedule, but we were young and invincible. We stood at the end of the trestle. We thought we were smart by putting our ears to the train track to ascertain if a train was coming.

"What we didn't know in our smartness was that we couldn't detect the vibrations since a large part of the track ran over the bridge and the vibrations stopped after leaving ground. Freddie stood and proceeded to walk out on the trestle. Past the middle, he took out a small can of red paint and a paint brush. Lying across one rail on his stomach he tried to paint his name upside down on the black supporting iron beam. Freddie wanted to be famous and as it turned out he was. Freddie was far out on the bridge so his painted name would be recognized. His concentration was so great he didn't hear me yelling. A train was barreling down the track. By the time Freddie realized his situation, he had only two options: run, hoping he could out distance the train or jump into the Gorge. Freddie started to run. His hands were reaching out for me as if I could pull him free. His eyes were wide with fear. He looked over his shoulder to see the Erie Lackawanna bearing down on him.

"The train's brakes shrieked, trying to slow thirty tons of steel. Freddie gave me one last look and jumped. I watched his fall: flaying arms, pumping legs, and a horrible scream. He hit the water with a big splash and never surfaced. It was a horrible moment that lives with me today. I still feel guilty that I couldn't do anything, that I should have done something before the accident. The train screeched to a stop. The police came. Freddie's parents marched up and down the Passaic River. Like Clancy, they finally found him at the bottom of Patterson Falls. I blamed the train. I blamed myself. But in the end, it was a terrible accident, nothing more.

"The very next week another friend, Jason, died when he was riding his bicycle—a drunk driver ran him over. And this was in the afternoon— an inebriated driver at midday of all things!

"So, Steve, do you think there was a conspiracy in all of this?"

"Well—no I guess not."

"There you go. Things sometimes are not what they appear to be. This is a nice neighborhood and, for the most part, I think safe. Martha and I never locked the house. Tend to your family and forget your ideas. Would you like some tea?"

Steve was too confused and murmured, "Sure."

"Excellent." Jack went to the kitchen to put on a pot of water.

Steve stood up, tired of sitting all day. He gazed around the dining room. Part of the living room was visible. He saw the few photos on the wall and was just starting to get a better view when Mr. Calhoun came back.

"It will be a few minutes till the water boils. So what have you been doing, Steve?"

"I have family, a wife and a five year old son and four year old daughter who keep me busy. My editor position at the *Echoes-Sentinel* is okay. I report on who took a vacation and where, marriages, Elk events, and local news. Nothing exciting."

"Nothing exciting. Why, I would imagine a conspiracy is exciting."

"Yes, it is. So you are saying that I am making this up to fill the void in my life?"

"Possibly. You haven't discovered anything so far, correct?"

"No. I was going by a gut intuition."

"Let it go, Steve." Jack went back into the kitchen.

Steve wanted to let it go, but he still had his suspicions even without evidence. The more people criticized him, the more he believed something was missing, something sinister.

Jack came back with a porcelain tea pot and cups decorated with pink flowers and green vines.

"You know, Steve? Real tea comes from a particular plant, Camellia Sinensis, a shrub native to China and India and there are only four varieties: green, black, white, and oolong. Anything else, like herbal 'tea,' is a mixture of a different plant and isn't technically tea. And real tea has antioxidants which can help with cancer, heart disease, and diabetes. Substitute teas don't have that. It's almost a lesson in life. Often the real is diffused by the fake. This happens to be green tea, one of my favorites."

Steve didn't particularly like tea, but wanted to be polite and carefully sipped the hot liquid. He had had too much tea for one day and nursed the cup in front of him.

Banter about the Township and new building restrictions occupied an hour, a time Steve felt was appropriate before leaving. The Troop was never brought up.

"Okay, thanks, Mr. Calhoun, for your time."

"Call me Jack. And come any time. I like company."

Steve found himself on the cottage porch, still nowhere near any solutions in this quixotic quest. Large gray clouds again covered the entire sky.

The streets were quiet. People had deserted the Millington Station Cafe in their journey to towns east, the

New York Pennsylvania Station or Hoboken Terminals.

The dreariness of the afternoon seeped into his emotions.

Determined to finish his research, despite the useless interviews, Steve drove to the *Echoes-Sentinel* office. Using an antiqued microfiche machine, he searched newspaper archives for serial killer articles over the last ten years in Long Hill Township and came up empty. He did find articles about Frederick Macoun and Jason Cohen that verified Mr. Calhoun's stories.

Then a final search of the largest newspaper in the stat—*Newark Star Ledger*. Again nothing about serial killings in this area.

A numbness overcame Steve. Perhaps he was wrong. Maybe, just maybe he was in need of psychiatric help. At his cluttered desk, Steve questioned how he came to be obsessed with the murders, finally grabbing on to his training to be a reporter, even though it was informal training at the *Sentential*. His love of writing and lack of any employable skills moved him to work at the newspaper after graduation. His major at Seton Hall University had been Norse Mythology: a useless study, but interesting. He was one of the few who dared to take it on and, if nothing else, he now understood how Norse mythology underpinned political behavior today— worthless knowledge that found no employment outside academia but was an individual triumph of investigation and perseverance.

So maybe that's what was driving him—the personal desire to find the truth and something meaningful in his life. Report and investigate a big story. Steve began to feel better about himself. Similar to digging into the old Norse myth of Ragnarok to determine if the catastrophic global climate experience was the same as now as it had been then or plodding through the *Edda,* which was written in Iceland a century after the close of the Viking Age, to establish if it was the source of Norse mythology. It was the writing, work, and the investigation that attracted him, not hallucinations. Just because there weren't any serial killings didn't mean there couldn't be one now. This was a unique situation, therefore a great opportunity. Steve relaxed. Yes, there probably was something to the killings that others, including the police, were not seeing and it was his job to find it.

After a big sigh of relief, he began writing about the wonderful experiences the Lembricks had on their vacation to Greece—a land of other gods.

Chapter 9

The Chester Lions Club created a weekend flea market on Route 206 on an open field straddling Chester Borough twenty miles north from Long Hill Township. During a fifteen-year period, the market became known state-wide, attended by thousands. Proceeds of vendor space rentals went to Lions free eye and hearing screenings and camps for the blind.

Paul liked to wander the Chester Flea Market each Sunday unaware of the charitable purpose. It was five acres of commercial items, garage junk, furniture, food, and the occasional treasure. The best thing was that most of the vendors were ignorant of the real worth of anything valuable they might be selling. Though his house was full of antiques, there was always room for a special item when found, like the eighteenth century oak dresser he recently purchased.

Paul preferred that Peter accompany him on these trips, but Peter was on call at the hospital. Still the hunt was exciting.

Paul shouldered his Visconti oiled distressed leather messenger shoulder bag for small items and had a check book for the big buys to be picked up later. Wearing a Ralph Lauren custom fit pink mercerized polo and hound's-tooth checked slacks, Paul felt far above all the average people in attendance today.

The sky was clear and the air mild—a perfect day for antiquing. Though it was autumn, the Chester Lions had extended the event for a couple of weeks more, due to this excellent weather. Before him was the meadow surrounded by colorful trees and occupied with hundreds of sellers.

Paul had a plan for these visits. He would walk the middle path in the meadow looking right and left for what each row had to offer. CDs, tooth paste and brushes, used clothing, comic books, toys, crafts, costume jewelry, fragrances, and food stands were quickly ignored. The atmosphere was alive with loud music from vinyl record sellers, hucksters with microphones, speakers exclaiming their wares, and the general noise of all those attending. Finding nothing worth looking at, Paul reached the end of the field and turned right to explore the vendors on the perimeter.

Usually furniture was on the outside because it was easier to load and unload.

Brushing at the horse flies near his head, which had wandered from the nearby horse farm lured by the smell of the food sellers, he continued his search.

On the right ahead, Paul spied an antique watch chain and bloodstone fob laying on a mahogany banquet along with cheap glassware and silver plated utensils. On their first year anniversary of living together, Paul had given Peter a large silver and gold dial Verge hunter pocket watch by Ferderer. The hunter case had a hinged bezel, back and front cover. The dial was decorated with engine turning and had a pair of gold hands and a blue steel sub second hand.

The front cover popped open to ninety degrees when the button was pressed. The fob would complement the watch. It might be expensive, but his relationship with Peter was more valuable.

And this was just the right thing for Peter. Paul couldn't believe how lucky he was. He started looking at the glassware not wanting to give away his interest in the fob. Finally picking up the fob, he asked about it.

"This very special," said the bald vendor, "made in England at the turn of the century." He emphasized the age. "This silver watch fob and chain was made in London in 1899 .The chain is twelve and one half inches long and in excellent condition. Each link is stamped. It's sterling silver and hallmarked. The bloodstone is two inches by one and a fourth inch with a total weight of seventy grams. The fob is in excellent condition."

Paul was excited. The date of production matched the date of the watch he had given Peter. He began to bicker with the vendor. The bald man sized up Paul, looking at his man bag and his expensive clothes and knew that he had money to spend. The asking price was set at two hundred and fifty dollars. Paul knew the real value was closer to three hundred and fifty dollars. Still, he bargained, liking the game. He could judge the ignorance of the vendor by his look and eagerness—shifty eyes, tongue licking the upper lip, position of the body. All this indicated the man wanted badly to sell.

As he was pressing the seller enjoying his superiority, a horse fly buzzed close to his cheek. "Damn flies!" was the last thing Paul uttered.

The vendor turned his head left to see what went by so fast. A nick in the tent pole and a small hole through the side canvas was new. Curious, but he had a sale to complete.

As the vendor turned back to Paul and held up the chain and fob so Paul could have a closer look, Paul's forehead exploded discharging brain matter, bone, and blood throughout the seller's tent.

"Damn!" said the seller before he realized what exactly had happened.

Paul tilted forward, hit his head on the table, leaving a wet spongy mass. His knees buckled and he fell back, face up, outside the tent. Eye sockets filled with thick blood. His pink polo deepened to red. The color expanded and seeped onto the grass.

The emergency medical technicians arrived in five minutes after the blood splattered vendor ran to their station in the meadow. Paul was pronounced dead at the scene. Chester Police arrived fifteen minutes later. Paul's body was quickly wrapped up and moved from the flea market. The police immediately came to a conclusion that a misplaced turkey hunter in the woods was too near the flea market and the buckshot had reached the vendor's stall. A search of the area produced no hunters or signs of turkey. Despite these peculiarities and the fact that later the coroner's office didn't find any spent buckshot in Paul's body, the incident was deemed an accident. The police didn't have a metal detector, so the case was quickly closed to prevent any lasting damage to the flea market. No one thought to search the grass aisles.

಄಄಄

It seemed that Paul was always the quiet one and did no harm, but he was a queer and was a member of the Troop. He never really came to the aid of others during the cruel jokes and harassing. At a hundred yards, it took two shots shot, but still better than anyone in the Troop could ever produce.

One more down.

The power of selecting death was intoxicating. I never felt as good as I do now. This almost made up for losing Clancy.

ↄ⁄ↄↄ

ACCIDENTAL OR INTENTIONAL?
By Stephen Mazur

Long Hill Township—It's time all residents should know of the three deaths within the last six months, three deaths involving former members of Millington Boy Scout Troop 186. Accidental or intentional? Let's take a look at the facts.

Kenneth Richardson, Clancy Dickerson, and Paul Moody died within a period of a few months.

Mr. Richardson was run over by a car, a car that actually rode on the sidewalk of New York City for some distance before it hit him. In fact, observers saw the car move out of a parking spot up the street and speed up, targeting Mr. Richardson. Richardson was an upcoming lawyer with Daley, Ryan & Forthsmith. He was a lifelong resident of Long Hill and engaged to marry Deborah Wallingford also of the Township.

Someone tried to poison Mr. Dickerson with rat poison in vanilla ice cream before he was brutally shoved down the Millington Gorge to drown. Though police linked intoxication to the "accident," Clancy Dickerson never drank hard liquor. Dickerson's family had lived on Long Hill Road for several generations. He is survived by his brother, Gordon.

Mr. Moody was shot in the head while at the Lions' Flea Market in Chester. This was no accident, despite what police think. Hunters wouldn't be near such a large crowd and turkeys would shy away by the noise and human activity. Moody too was a lifelong resident of this area and was partnered with Peter Weber.

Our police department didn't find any evidence at the death sites for Mr. Dickerson or Mr. Moody. But this reporter went to the gorge where Mr. Dickerson was supposedly drunk and slipped. I found a half-eaten bagel near the edge. I knew Mr. Dickerson; he would not drop food unless he was under duress and he didn't drink. He had a black grease mark on the back of his shirt. Where did this come from? Mr. Dickerson was impeccable with his clothing.

This reporter also went to the flea market a day after the murder and searched the grounds behind the vendor stand where Mr. Moody was

*in the process of purchasing a watch fob. I found
a .22 spent bullet in the grassy isle by the stand.
Rifles aren't allowed for hunting in the State of
New Jersey. This first round clearly came from a
shooter, not a hunter!*

*Mr. Moody was a quiet introspective per-
son. I doubt many knew him. He was never upset
or hostile to anyone. Who would kill such a
man?*

*Obviously, the police weren't as adept as
they could have been. While this evidence isn't
conclusive, it undoubtedly should be looked into.
I gave the bullet and the half-eaten bagel to the
police for further investigation. Perhaps DNA
and bullet striations will move these investigations forward. So far, this reporter hasn't heard
from our law enforcers. The lack of progress in
solving these cases seems suspicious to many local residents. At the time of this printing, the
coroner's report for Mr. Dickerson has not been
made public. The report for Mr. Moody was
clearly a rush job to save the reputation of the
Chester Flea Market. I hope, with my finding, it
will be re-opened. We need the truth!*

*If we have a serial killer or multiple killers
in our community, a thorough investigation must
begin now by our township police or the state
troopers. We cannot wait for another killing,*

certainly not since Peter Weber and I are the only remaining former members of Troop 186. And after these Scouts are gone, who is next?

Residents should be cautious, making sure they have a way to check the front door without answering, or use a side window or other means to check on visitors. Be aware of your surroundings and be alert to anything suspicious. Our quiet neighborhoods have undergone a radical change!

If you have any information on these deaths, please step forward and contact this reporter (smazur@msn.com) or the police. As a community we must not panic, but must work cohesively to solve these murders. Above all, be alert and watch your backs!

Steve brought his article to the managing editor of the *Echoes-Sentinel*.

"This time it has to be printed. Our readers need to know."

The managing editor read the article. "Don't you think you are too hard on our police department?"

"Hard? They did a crappy job of investigating each death. They would rather be in a car eating a donut watching for speeders than do a lot of hump work."

"We don't want a confrontation with the police."

"So what kind of newspaper is this? A gossip rag? If

we don't print it, I'll take it to the *Newark Star Ledger*. Nothing locally has been made public about these deaths. Our readership needs to be informed. Isn't that what we really are about?"

The managing editor tilted his chair back and thought. The *Echoes-Sentinel* had once been a viable newspaper, churning out real news and information. It had lost its luster some years ago and now relied on coupons, anniversaries, birthdays, and charitable events for news, but community stories made people feel comfortable. Hard news could be disruptive. The morning TV news programs were more of a circus than investigative and informative. People needed a reassuring medium to retire to from the frenzy of life.

"I don't know."

"What is the *Echoes-Sentinel* then?"

The managing editor looked at the article once more. Maybe, just maybe, this was a chance to get into the mainstream of real newspaper reporting again. Maybe it was time for the *Echoes-Sentinel* to step out of the supermarket racks and free distribution on everyone's lawn and into the coin operated newspaper vending machines and in-store racks, like the better-established broadsheets. And with this, he would grow with the paper. So he would start small and see how the community handled this. "Well, it isn't a large piece. Perhaps, we can place it on page two and see how it rolls. I hope it doesn't inflame our readers."

Steve was about to object to a second page place-ment, but quickly realized that he had won and the article would be published. "Fine. Great." He left the room in a good mood, feeling like a real newspaper editor.

The article came out the next morning and so did the police.

The general secretary of the newspaper walked an officer in the large staff room where Steve sat at his desk.

"Mr. Mazur?" inquired Lieutenant Matthew Arnold.

Steve leaned forward not inviting Lieutenant Arnold to sit. "Yes, how may I help you?"

Arnold wasn't a big man, but he carried himself as if he were. His brown hair was military cut and his uniform crisp. Steel-rimmed glasses gave an austere appearance and the brim of a polished hat visor covered the upper part of green eyes so he was masked and hard to read.

After he had passed a written exam, a physical agili-ty test, comprehensive background investigation, oral in-terviews, medical and psychological examinations, and drug testing, Matthew Arnold was hired as a patrolman by Long Hill Township due to a retirement vacancy. Up-on completing academy training in Parsippany, he was sworn in by State Assemblyman Albert Merck. Arnold advanced to sergeant then to lieutenant. But he was more than the initial requirements and subsequent promotions. He was a troubled man who needed to constantly prove his worth.

Law enforcement gave him an edge over others he

hadn't possessed before and he used it. His stature of being a senior law enforcer defined his life.

While he never considered himself a bully, Arnold was strongly assertive and opinionated, using his shield to hide any doubt that may present itself. He would never admit to the weakness of needing help. The position of chief was open and he planned to have it. These incidents would be the key to success. He had only to progress with caution, and within standard procedures, to solve the case. This small town reporter wasn't going to disrupt that. "I want to talk about the article you wrote in today's paper."

The staff near Steve became quiet while pretending to continue work.

"Okay, do you have any information about the killings?"

"Well, first you call them 'murders' and we don't know that they are. Second, you put our police department in a bad light. I will not have that."

"Have you really investigated any of these deaths thoroughly? Have you done anything with the bullet I found?"

"Mr. Mazur, we take every infraction of the law seriously and do a methodical job of investigating. We are looking into the bullet, but it does not necessarily tie in with the demise of Mr. Moody. It could have been there a long time. You do not need to tell me how to run the force. I resent the way you depicted us in the paper."

"Lieutenant, I am merely reporting the facts."

"You came to a decision too quickly about this being a serial killer. A serial killer can be defined as a person who enjoys luring, attacking, and killing his victims based on an established ritual—an established ritual. Do you see any ritual in these deaths?"

"Well, no."

"Furthermore, we can't profile the entire population of Long Hill Township for persons who were cruel to animals, had bed wetting beyond toilet training, suffered extended psychological abuse, fantasize about holding total control, or have dysfunctional relationships that would enforce isolation and solitude. These are the traits of a serial killer, Mr. Mazur. We will study each death and the people surrounding it to determine if there is indeed a serial killer. So far, we haven't found any fibers or fingerprints for each event. You don't need to infuse fear in the community or, worse, alert the serial killer, if there is one, as we develop our findings and advance this forward."

"Lieutenant, I report the facts."

"Just make sure they are facts and not the imaginings of a bored second-rate reporter. Good day, sir."

Lieutenant Matthew Arnold marched out of the room, quickly followed in by the managing editor.

"What did he say?"

"That they are on the job and my article was an insult to the department."

"I told you so. However, we've had a huge demand for more papers this morning so we are running a second issue. When you have legitimate facts, we'll print another article."

Steve looked at the back of the managing editor as he left. No back bone in that one. Now that he knew the police department was not pursuing a vigorous investigation, it was up to him to discover the truth.

c∂c∂

They don't know! They don't know! The article by Mazur was pitiful, but he had to be more careful, now that all of Long Hill Township was alerted. He needed to pick the next victim carefully. He had never felt so good, so elated. This was better than booze.

c∂c∂

The day was blanketed by thin gray clouds. Rain could fall whenever it wished.

On his way to Mr. Calhoun's house seeking a Troop membership list, Steve drove past Clancy's home. Two Weichert Realtors sales signs were placed on the massive front lawn. For a fleeting moment, Steve wondered what had happened to Gordon.

Past Tim Hardy's abandoned garage, Steve spied a wonderful old blue car in the partially opened first bay and tried to guess who it belonged to. No one he knew, certainly.

Steve pulled into Mr. Calhoun's driveway. He hoped Mr. Calhoun kept records. Perhaps, there was someone that was in the Troop he had forgotten. He had to follow all leads like a true investigative reporter.

Jack greeted Steve. "What an interesting article you wrote."

"Just trying to find the answers, Mr. Calhoun."

"Please, I asked you to call me Jack. Do you still think we have a serial killer running loose in the Township?"

"Okay, Jack. I'm still investigating all options. May I come in?"

"Certainly."

Again Jack guided Steve into the dining room. The aroma of Jack Daniels and pipe tobacco waffled in from the living room.

"What can I do for you now, my boy?"

"Do you have a list of all the member of Troop 186?"

"All the members? What year?"

"Just the years I was in the Troop."

"I'll have to look. Do you want it now?"

"If possible."

Jack went into another room. Steve could hear paper rustling and drawers opening. He spent the time gazing around the dining room, wondering if Jack had a wife. As a Scout, Jack never mentioned being married and Steve never saw him with any woman. The interior seemed tidy enough, but time seemed to have stopped in this house. The decor and everything in the room seemed to be late 'fifties. After only fifteen minutes, he heard a faint "Ah."

"Here they are." Jack handed Steve a battered folder.

"Thank you, Jack. May I take this? I'll be sure to return it."

"You can take it, provided you tell me first what, if anything, you discover."

"No problem."

Steve left with a purpose into a light drizzle.

ℰℐℰℐ

Giovanni read the *Echoes-Sentinel* and became mad that his name wasn't incorporated with the Troop. They had forgotten about him, but perhaps it was a good thing. Unconsciously, he touched the scar on his cheek. Everyone was talking about this crappy article and looking over their shoulders. It wasn't good to be public, especially if you had a record.

At the age of eighteen, he had tried to rob the Stirling Hardware store with a toy gun, but botched that and served eighteen months in the Morris County Correctional Facility.

He didn't think it was fortunate that the Inn took him back, since no one really wanted this job, except the desperate. No other business would employ him in the town. Without a car and expendable cash, Giovanni was doomed to his fate.

He dumped powdered soap into the sink and turned on the hot water. Giovanni was always fascinated by the growing bubbles. It seemed each phosphorescent globe was its own world, perhaps a world where he could do whatever he wanted and would contain friends, lots of friends.

The water was too hot to handle so Giovanni stepped outside to wait for it to cool a little and almost fell over the tavern's mongrel lying by the doorstep. A swift kick to the dog's belly sent it on its way. He searched through the kitchen rubble and found his bottle of Jack Daniels: a respite from his miserable world.

He never really fit in. Perhaps it was his short stature, swarthy looks, and the accent he couldn't get rid of. He was brought to America when he was seven by an uneducated father and meek mother. Their life was less than pleasant. They lived with his uncle in one room sharing the kitchen and bathroom.

He started to work part time at the age of twelve, washing dishes at the Stirling Inn to help support the family. His father never had a full time job, just daily contract work for lawn maintenance and minor home repairs. Giovanni had remained at the Inn all this time, even when his parents died, never getting a promotion or praise for the work he was doing. The hotel provided room and board which kept his earnings low, but gave a center to his life. His lack of education, criminal record, and even his accent prevented him from better employment, not only in this town, but probably in the entire State of New Jersey. He certainly didn't want to follow in his father's footsteps, begging for menial jobs. At least he had a regular paycheck. Giovanni was stuck in time at the Stirling Inn.

He had always been last—in class, in picking teams in gym, and life in general. Back then, he thought that by joining the Troop, he would be included as an equal and a genuine part of something, but the way the Scouts treated him was too much to bear. They weren't true Scouts!

The Boy Scout slogan still burned in his head: "Do a Good Turn Daily!" Yeah, Sure.

Now he had the pleasure of them dying, one by one. The Troop should have remembered the Scout Motto as well: "Be Prepared!" Richardson, Dickerson, and Moody weren't. So finally something good had come his way.

ೞೞೞ

Jack Calhoun sat in the living room with the late afternoon shadows sneaking through the front window blinds. The present life he had was declining bit by bit. Nothing to do now, except to mark the days gone past. The wall was his timeline. It had first given him some meaning to life, but when his wife died, he removed her photo from the wall. He decided not to live in the past, but make every day significant—a positive attitude. That was hard to do and in the end he gave up. He walked in a slight daze, a path of routines occupying his day from waking to sleeping.

Looking at the wall where photos of his wife, his brother, Kenny, Clancy, and Paul used to be, Jack finally realized that the absence of the photos didn't help to forget and move on. They only added to his misery.

Meeting with Steve merely brought up forgotten dark memories of sitting in corners with a bottle of Jack Daniels while the Troop did who knew what. He was a terrible Scout Leader. The Troop did occupy his time, but it wasn't a quality experience and proved to be far worse.

A light breeze filtered through the room.

"Damn it, I forgot to close the window again," Jack muttered.

He had always opened it a crack to get some cool night air into the house. Jack slowly rose from the floral wingback recliner, shuffled over to the window, and slid the pane down, but didn't lock it—he and his wife never did. After all, they did live in a safe community and the bother of locking and unlocking seemed unnecessary.

Now that he was up, Jack decided he would make his weekly run to ShopRite to refill the nearly empty pantry and refrigerator. He shuffled to the hall coat closet and opened the door to retrieve his hat. It was a rather warm day so he didn't need a coat.

As he turned to leave, a figure emerged from behind the coats in the right side of the closet, wrapped a knotted scout neckerchief around Jack's throat, and pulled both ends tight.

Jack couldn't even gag, so taut was the hold. The knot pressed deep. His now-blood-red eyes bulged as the garrote tightened. Facial capillaries ruptured, producing tiny red spots on his face. He tried to rip the garrote off but couldn't get his fingers under the cloth. He reached for the assailant's face.

His feet slipped on the polished wooden floorboards as he tried to disable the attacker. Falling only make the grip more rigid. Within a few seconds, Jack was unconscious and slumped to floor, taking the mugger with him, but the choke hold remained firm for another five minutes to make sure the effort was successful. A surgical gloved finger touch Jack's carotid artery as an extra precaution.

Jack was now with his wife. The neckerchief was slipped off.

The attacker thought for a moment then dropped the neckerchief on Jack's face and left as silently as he had entered, through the window.

Jack wasn't found for three weeks. The heavy order of the decaying body finally found access to the street outside by another open window.

If it had color, it would have been green and rust brown. The aroma of death slowly drifted with the breeze, eventually permeating the Millington Station Cafe. The owners weren't pleased. Tracking the smell led to Jack.

The autopsy examined all of the tissues of the neck, superficial and deep, and tracked the force vector that produced the injuries—suffocation.

Patterned abrasions and contusions of the skin of the anterior on his decomposed flesh vaguely revealed abrasions on his neck caused by his fingernails.

This time the conclusion was murder by strangulation. The police even had the weapon—a Boy Scout neckerchief.

❡❡❡

This made up for the loss of Dickerson. Good riddance to an old man who cared nothing for the boys he was charged with.

This time, it was more rewarding to actually sense death creep into Mr. Calhoun's body and feel the constriction of flesh as I pulled tighter and tighter. Leaving the neckerchief was genius.

Now, now everyone would know it was only one person—me, finally recognition! The whole area would be in fear because of me. Such power, such power! I couldn't help but giggle as I planned again.

❡❡❡

MURDER IN MILLINGTON
By Stephen Mazur

Millington – This reporter's account of a serial killer in the Township is now verified with the demise of Mr. Jack Calhoun, former Scout Leader of Troop 186. Township Police responded to a call from the Millington Station Café about an odorous smell. The stench led to Mr. Calhoun's house. The front door was unlocked. Upon entering Sergeant Jay Molosic found Calhoun face down in the hall near a closet. There was no evidence of forced entry and no motive was immediately present. Nothing seemed stolen and the only signs of struggle were Mr. Calhoun's scuff marks on the wooden floor. The interior of the house was unmolested. The killer had come for only one thing: the death of Calhoun and immediately left after it was accomplished.

Mr. Calhoun was pronounced dead at the scene. The autopsy revealed that he had been brutally strangled five days past.

As I have reported, three members of Troop 186 had died under suspicious circumstances recently. More importantly a Boy Scout neckerchief was found at the site of Calhoun's demise linking all these four deaths. To all appearanc-

es, it seems someone, perhaps multiple persons, is tracking down each member of this Scout Troop. But why? Why wait all these years to extract revenge, jealously or some other impetus.

For full disclosure, I was a member of Troop 186; therefore I have more interest in these events than just reporting news.

No motivation was evident for each murder. The only common bond was membership in the Troop. This reporter visited Mr. Calhoun recently and received a list of scout names during the period that Mr. Richardson, Mr. Dickerson, and Mr. Moody were active members.

For the safety of all, these are the names of the surviving Scouts living in Long Hill Township:

Steve Mazur

Peter Weber

Theodore Nestor and Gary Wilton were "part time" members and rarely attended meetings. Russell Baker and Samuel Voles were also members for a limited time before moving out-of-state. I don't remember Baker or Voles and, so far, I have not been able to contact them.

These two Township residents are in danger of being the next victim. I urge our law enforcers to provide protection for these men and their families.

The term, serial killer, was created in the mid-1970s by Robert Ressler, the director of the FBI's Violent Criminal Apprehension Program. Mr. Ressler grew up watching serial movies. Before he used this term this horrific events were called mass murders or stranger-on-stranger crimes.

The police in England called multiple murders, "crime in a series."

Serial murders are not a new phenomenon. They occur in ancient and modern times i.e. Locusta of Gaul who murdered thousands by poison in the mid-first century CE, Robert Lee Yates who killed 13 women in Spokane, Washington, Gary Ridgway the Green River Killer - the most prolific serial killer in U.S., and of course Jack the Ripper. However, serial killers are rare. The FBI reports they account for less than one percent of all murders. Serial killers have defined geographic areas of operation: they conduct their murders within comfort zones. We have not had a homicide in the Township till this rash of deaths – now we have four in a short space of time. The Township appears to be a comfort zone for the killer. This should send up red flags in the Police Department.

I believe we have a Missionary Serial Killer—a person who feels a responsibility to elimi-

nate a certain group of people. There really is not profile for this type of killer. He could be a husband with a family, a professor, or the mailman. She could be a housewife with children, a teacher, or a lawyer. He or she could be your neighbor and you will never know till it is too late.

So again, I caution residences not to take this lightly. Because you were not part of Troop 186, does not mean you are safe. Until we actually know the motivation(s) of this killer, all are in danger. Is there another link to these murders than just the Scout Troop? Think about it and be aware and safe.

Steve sat back in his chair after reading his article on the *Echoes-Sentinel's* front page. It was better than the first—more research and more grabbing lines. Best of all, the *Newark Star Ledger* or other bigger papers than the *Sentinel* hadn't caught on to these serial murders yet. The story was all his.

Steve was feeling fine and then Lieutenant Arnold marched into the room.

"What did I tell you about defaming our police department?"

"I wasn't maligning the department, Lieutenant. As I told you, I merely report the facts and I don't see our police doing much."

"That's because it takes time to thoroughly investigate, time we seem to have precious little of now."

"How much time?"

"As long as it takes. And you might be interested to learn that we caught the killer of Mr. Dickerson."

At this, Steve bolted up. "What?"

"We apprehended the killer due to good police work. It seems your serial killer theory is all wind and no substance."

"Well, who is the killer?"

"Tim Hardy."

"Tim Hardy?"

"Yes, he wanted the Model L. In the brief conversations, he had with Mr. Dickerson, he learned that the car was kept secret for fear of robbery so no one knew about it. Hardy badly wanted the antique. We traced greasy palm and finger marks on the back of Mr. Dickerson's shirt. Luckily, Hardy had a minor criminal record for stealing as a teenager so we could match them. We also found surgical gloves covered with Jack Daniels in the trash container in the back of the garage. So you can see, Mr. Mazur, we are doing our duty."

Steve was stunned. His theory was blown again. He had been so sure. Grasping for straws, "Could you link Hardy to the other murders?"

"No. He had no connections with Mr. Richardson, Mr. Moody, or Mr. Calhoun. Hardy admitted to only killing Mr. Dickerson. I would appreciate you mentioning our efforts in your next column." Lieutenant Arnold made a crisp turn around and walked out of the office.

Steve wasn't so sure there would be another article.

❧❧❧

Don Gold had been preparing for calamity and crisis since he had moved here from Newark after the 1967 demonstrations, looting, and destruction left twenty-six dead and hundreds injured. Race riots in Rochester, Harlem, Philadelphia, and Watts had convinced him that the inevitable end of days was forthcoming. As an early survivalist, he actively prepared for emergencies, including possible disruptions in social or political order, on scales from local to international. This was one of the situations he had been planning for.

He read Mazur's article for a second time, especially the two sentences, *Because you were not part of Troop 186, does not mean you are safe. Until we actually know the motivation(s) of this killer, all are in danger.*

The message was clear and correct: dark days were coming. The fabric of civilization was starting to unwind. He must now be on high alert for unusual activity and suspicious of everyone, including friends and acquaintances. A person that was once trusted could very well be the one that was the serial killer.

This was the time to remain reclusive and on defense.

Don had thinning hair, wore steel-rimmed glasses, and only measured five feet, two inches. Preparing for the unforeseen made up for his stature. In this, he was the superior person and would outlive all others.

Don opened a fortified locked door in the kitchen and went to his cellar to inspect his emergency stockpile. The windows were cinder blocked. A generator with exhaust pipes hidden under rose bushes lit the room to reveal walls of food grade water containers, freeze dried food, boxes of canned vegetables and soups, bottles of vitamins, propane camping stove, and other survival necessities. What he was interested in at this particular moment, was the triple locked steel cabinet containing weapons to defend him against intruders—a 12-gauge pump shotgun, best for close quarter home defense since aiming didn't have to be accurate; an AR-15, the best automatic rifle for outside invaders with a higher capacity of ammunition; a .45 semi-automatic pistol, best for concealment and easy to handle; pepper spray; and a Taser Public Defender stun gun.

The AR-15, .45 pistol, and the stun gun were bought with the help of Sergeant Molosic who had them smuggled in from Pennsylvania.

Don checked the magazine of the .45 and then placed the pistol under his belt in back. He wasn't defenseless like the others. He was ready.

Gold stayed inside over the weekend and didn't go out for the following three days. He kept guard by a front window, observing every car and resident that passed by. He was sure another killing would occur soon and then the riots demanding action and protection would begin. He had seen this happen in Newark. Don was smart. He didn't just watch the front. He watched all sides of the house. As a precaution, he set up GE personal keychain alarm trip wires around the perimeters. When crossed, the trip wire would pull a pin out of the keychain activating an internal alarm. Always the perfectionist, Don made a rain jacket from the corners of sandwich bags and placed them over each key chain to shed any rain. No one would sneak up on him.

Don didn't call his office to inform them of his absence—why announce he was alone? Someone in the office could be the killer as well. Long Hill Township was a small place and rumors quickly ran their circuit. Best to be quiet till it was over.

He would only venture outside at night for the *Echoes- Sentinel* thrown on his lawn by the paper boy. The grass grew and weeds poked through the thorny rose bushes. Don didn't care. This was a crisis situation.

The staff at the Robert Montross Insurance Group in Morristown began to worry about Don after the third day he was absent. Phone calls to the house weren't answered.

Don was a withdrawn person, never joined in office lunch room discussions, never attended a Montross event, and never invited anyone to his house. The staff concern was not over Don's well-being. Paper work was piling up and no one wanted to take on the added responsibility of completing it.

"Someone should go to his house," Michele, the office receptionist, suggested on a noon time break.

"Maybe the serial killer got him," Brian, senior manager of the office, proposed lightly.

"Nonsense. This is all hype to sell newspapers." said George, a former college football player and now the personal lines agent.

"Well, I haven't read anything about it in the *Star Ledger*."

"Listen, Brian, this serial killer story is made up. Sure, there have been deaths, more than normal, but no reason to jump to wild conclusions."

"Well, George, why don't you go to Don's house and find out what's up?"

"Me?"

"Yes, you. You're the nearest to a friend that Don had here."

"I just joked with him, actually at him, that's all."

"That's enough. Do you want me to suggest to Mr. Knots that you take up his work?"

"Couldn't we just call the police department?"

"We don't know if it serious. Don just may be sick."

The other two stared at him.

"Okay, okay, I'll go after work tonight."

By the time George finished contacting potential customers and analyzing current existing coverage for his clients, who requested it, it was late and dark outside. He thought of putting off a visit to Don, but knew Michele would give him trouble in the morning.

The night was misty and a light rain fell. Clouds partially covered the moon so it looked like the *Star Wars'* death star. George had just viewed the movie with his fiancé so he envisioned this as a quest. It was much better than just going to see if this miserable man was alive.

George arrived at Don's house in a half hour and parked along the road. Ignoring the long path to the house on his far right, George hunched down in the rain and walked on the lawn directly to the front door. He quickly tripped a wire. A 120 decibel ear piercing sound went off.

The front door opened a crack. "Who is that?"

George couldn't hear Don and was slightly dazed by the resonance of the alarm.

"Who goes there?" Don inquired again, peering into the night.

George stumbled forward and, upon seeing Don behind the door, began waving his arms. Perhaps just seeing him was enough. No, everyone would want an explanation. George persisted on.

"Stop!"

George's black coat and Indiana Jones wide brimmed hat made him a menacing-looking figure at night. The partial moon was behind his back, silhouetting his broad, bent-forward outline.

"Stop!"

The alarm was still blaring as George kept coming forward hoping to get out of the rain and wishing he had taken the path. His black Florsheim Brookside shoes weren't damp, they were wet. Why had he come?

Don removed the 45 from his back and took aim.

"We thought you were ill or worse dead," called George through the noise.

Don only heard the word "dead" through the shrill and fired a single shot. One was all that was needed. George's head nodded back and he gently fell on rose bushes with a perfectly round hole in his forehead. The back of his head was not as neat.

Neighbors heard the alarm and subsequent shot. Some rushed over to Don's house, while others began to phone the police that the serial killer was about.

Don saw a small group of people descending on his homestead. The social order was also in chaos—the riots had begun!

They were coming for him and his weapons and supplies. Didn't they know he had eliminated the serial killer? He fired another shot into the air. The group screamed and ran in all directions. Don backed into his house and locked the door.

The police arrived ten minutes later with sirens wailing, adding to the chaos and clamor outside.

Two cars and a van screeched to a stop. Officers popped out in full riot gear. Lieutenant Arnold ordered some to surround the house, another to find the alarm and disable it. He brought forward a megaphone.

"Mr. Gold, please come out."

Ten minutes of silence and no motion.

An emergency medical technician had crept along the wet grass to the flattened rose bush and George. He signaled by waving a flat hand across his throat to Arnold that resuscitation was not needed.

"Mr. Gold, please come out."

The front window opened a crack. "I shot the serial killer!"

"Yes, now please step onto the porch so we can talk."

The door slowly opened and Don stepped forward still holding his 45.

"Put the gun down!"

"You don't understand. I'm a hero. I shot the serial killer." Don raised the 45 to show that he really did it."

Sergeant Molosic recognized Don and the Pennsylvania weapon he had sold him. A quick blast from his 9 mm brought Don to his knees.

"Who did that?" Arnold asked, and before any answer, he was running to the house. Behind him was a paramedic.

Don was sitting against the porch siding, watching a red stain slowly spread from his chest.

Arnold reached Don and looked back for the paramedic.

"What happened? I'm a hero. I don't understand."

"Relax, Mr. Gold." The lieutenant stepped back to allow the paramedic to do his work. He walked back to the squad cars. "Who fired?"

A brief moment of stillness before Molosic spoke. "I did."

"Why?"

"He was pointing the pistol. I—I thought he was going to shoot."

Arnold reflected for a moment: Molosic might be right on this one. The deadly force rule allowed police to use force when the situation was likely to cause serious bodily injury or death to another person. An investigation would prove if this was justified.

"Okay, leave your pistol and badge on my desk. You are officially on administrative leave till this is settled."

The ambulance drove the two men to Morristown Memorial. It arrived with two dead bodies.

Chapter 10

The next morning Lieutenant Arnold confronted Steve at the *Echoes- Sentinel* office.

"Do you know what has happened last night?"

"What do you mean?"

"Don Gold shot and killed George Neuman last night."

"Who is Don Gold? Who is George Neumann?"

"Mr. Gold was a resident of this community and Mr. Neumann was his work colleague."

"I don't know these people. What does this have to do with me or the serial killer?"

"Gold thought Mr. Neumann was the serial killer coming for him."

"Was he?"

"You don't understand, Mazur, Don was influenced by your articles. He was a 'prepper' and was paranoid. You put him over the edge!"

"Hey, hey. Don't blame me for other people's problems."

Lieutenant Arnold pointed his finger at Steve menacingly. "It *is* your problem. You are the cause."

"No, I just write the facts. I don't control how readers interpret it and certainly I'm not responsibility for what do they do."

"You're wrong, Mazur. You are causing panic and chaos in our small township. Almost daily we receive phones calls about suspicious figures lurking about, about neighbors and friends and we have to look into each one."

"It seems that this Gold event is outside the serial killings just like the Dickerson murder."

"People don't see it that way. Beware the power of the word. We don't have the manpower or time to divert us from legitimate investigations." The lieutenant tossed a slip of paper on Steve's desk. "By the way, this is a ticket for a broken tail light."

"I don't have a broken light."

"You do now. Be careful what you write."

TRAGEDY IN GILLETTE
By Stephen Mazur

Gillette: Mr. Don Gold, living on Summit Avenue, shot and killed George Neuman, his co-worker Tuesday night as Mr. Neuman walked over Gold's lawn to the front door. It was a rainy night with low visibility. Neuman crossed over a trip wire set up by Gold, causing a high-decibel alarm to sound. Mr. Neuman was a bachelor and has no surviving family.

Police surmised that Gold was under the supposition that Mr. Neuman was the serial killer since he looked menacing crouched over in the rain hiding his face. The loud noises prevented verbal communication and as Neuman kept moving forward, Mr. Gold became more fearful.

Mr. Neuman was a personal lines agent at the Montross Insurance Agency in Morristown where Mr. Gold was employed as an accountant. Neuman went to inquire about Gold's condition after he missed three consecutive days of work, did not answer calls, and did not report in.

Mr. Gold was a survivalist or "prepper." He had stock piles of goods and a cabinet of weapons in his fortified cellar. He lived alone. Mr. Gold was predisposed to expect violence against him. It was this state of mind that led to the tragic shooting.

Mr. Gold was shot in the stomach by the police as he stood on his porch, waving a 45 semi-automatic pistol in their direction and toward the crowd of neighbors who gathered before the house. Previously Gold had also fired into a crowd that had initially arrived because of the first shot and alarm noise. Fortunately, no one in the crowd was injured. Gold was pronounced dead at Morristown Memorial that night.

This sad mistake must not happen again. The deaths of Mr. Gold and Mr. Neuman are tragic and serve to remind us that citizens cannot take the law into their own hands. Please be aware of your surroundings during this stressful period. Be alert, be cautious, but do not take overt action. Call the police if you are threatened, suspect or see anything unusual.

In another incident, police announced a suspect in the Clancy Dickerson murder. Tim Hardy, owner of Hardy Repair in Millington, allegedly killed Mr. Dickerson to gain possession of a 1930 Model L Lincoln automobile owned by Dickerson. Palm and finger prints on the shirt of Mr. Dickerson matched Hardy's. Rubber gloves with residue of Jack Daniels were discovered in the dumpster behind the garage. Mr. Hardy finally admitted to killing Mr. Dickerson, thanks to effective police interrogation. He refused to admit to any other deaths, insisting he was not a multiple killer and didn't know or have any contact with other recent victims from Boy Scout Troop 186.

While this one confession may appear to weaken the serial killer theory, I remind readers that Mr. Hardy confessed to only one murder. The Kenneth Richardson, Paul Moody, and Jack Calhoun deaths are as yet unsolved and the only common link remains Troop 186.

This reporter still believes there is a serial killer roaming our Township. Surely Tim Hardy was hoping Dickerson's death would be blamed on the serial killer, but thanks to excellent police work, Hardy didn't get away with it.

It is in earnest that I urge everyone to remain calm but watchful and let our police department do its work.

Steve was satisfied with this piece. He kept his theory alive and placated the police. The research he did: interviewing neighbors, co-workers, even the police paid off.

It was a well-rounded article. He wondered what would happen next, with fear always in the back of his mind.

�@✰✪

Things were progressing, maybe not the way I wanted, but moving forward nonetheless. I have decided on
who will be next and it will be personal.

⁊⁊⁊

Morristown was the County Seat of Morris County
in which Long Hill Township resided. George Washington slept in Morristown as it served as his headquarters
for two different winter encampments during the Revolu-
tionary War.

Morristown was the birth place of a number of nota-
bles. Anna Harrison, wife of President William Henry
Harrison; Caroline C. Fillmore wife of President Millard
Fillmore; Gene Shalit, film critic; Linda Hunt, actress;
Steve Forbes, editor-in-chief of *Forbes*

Thomas Nast creator of the modern version of Santa
Claus lived in Morristown for twenty years. As the nearest hospital in the region was Morristown Memorial, the
serial killer might be included as another notable since he
was probably born there.

The Town had dignity and relegated the events in
Long Hill Township as unfortunate country folk behavior
since no murders had been recorded for years in this important county seat. Burglary was common, possibly because forgotten Morristown residents with incomes below
the poverty level far exceeded the entire State of New
Jersey.

One of the low income residents now was Gary Wilton Senior, who awoke from a disturbed sleep—not for the first time. It was dark. The closet room off the car bays he was in did not have a window. He turned on the table lamp on the floor by his cot and, in fumbling, slid his worn Bible across the floor. Picking it up and needlessly brushing it off, he carefully placed it near, arm's length, by the lamp and surveyed his dismal surroundings, remembering where he was and who he was. He had lived in the Salvation Army's Morristown homeless shelter till they hired him to repair the vehicles, motorcycles, lawnmowers, snow blowers, and boat engines that were donated and included this small room in the garage.

The Salvation Army was founded in 1852 by William Booth in England to preach the gospel to the poor and homeless. Its beliefs, rooted in the Methodist tradition, committed to spreading the good news of Jesus and this good news had deeply affected Gary.

Gary took particular interest in one of the army's doctrines: "We believe that God's creation of the universe was perfect, but when man first deliberately disobeyed God, sin and suffering entered the world. As a result, man's relationship with God has been spoiled."

For the first time in his life, he felt a part of something with a meaning to his life. The Salvation Army was his home and the people here treated him with Christian respect. For this, he read his Bible and dutifully attended Sunday worship.

Gary's mother was very religious and imparted the Word of God daily. As a youth, he ignored them. Now that he was alone, he sought refuge in the Lord. At seventeen, Gary impregnated the first girl that allowed him to come near. She was a drug addict, and like Gary's mother, she sought redemption in religion to relieve her from her miserable condition. The two became friends, but shortly after Junior's birth, she left.

His mother kept his father at bay during his drinking bouts. When his mother died, Gary experienced further suffering at home from his father. Finally his father passed and for a while, Gary lived peacefully with his son, Gary Junior.

As a troubled boy, Gary had hoped Troop 186 would accept and support him, but the Troop was cruel. Gary doggedly stayed with them, hoping it was just an initiation phase. It wasn't and he found the Troop acted as if they were under the umbrella of All Saints' Episcopal Church, but they just used the Church for their own means, blaspheming against God All Mighty!

Thinking about the Troop made Gary very mad. Unconsciously, he rubbed his bent arm. Dreaming of the Troop murders made Gary realize that past evil was being avenged. God would triumph over the wicked.

He had just moved to this small room on Spring Street in the army's main loading bays. Some of his few belonging he brought were still boxed, but he didn't want to open them anymore. Though small, the room was his and he didn't have to endure the snoring in the homeless shelter.

Gary had to use the men's restroom in the main building where he was located. It had been awhile since his last bath at the Mission. His face was permanently impregnated with oil and grease from years of engine work.

Dark lines filled crevices on his cheeks and rested under his eyes giving him either a tortured Christ look or tormented demon appearance. Thanks to the cologne contributed by donors to the army, he maintained what he considered to be a respectable appearance.

He took advantage of the Salvation Army's food pantry or ate at the Market Street Mission off Route 202. It was a simple life, not worthy, but became purposeful after he finally found his life's obligation to God.

Gary sat up. He forgot how long it was between underwear changes. His crumpled clothes lay on the partially blue painted concrete floor. A quick smell assured him they were still all right to wear.

The assignment clipboard rattled on its hook on the outside door panel as Gary stepped into the bays. Since it was Saturday, he didn't bother to look at it.

The light that tried to make it into the bays from overhead door cracks was muted and fuzzy. It wasn't strong enough to penetrate into Gary's room. It was as if some force refused it permission. A rat scurried along the opposite bay floor. He had managed thus far to keep the rats away from his room, though some gained access to the army's store of donated food.

Two ghostly white vans were parked in the bays along with a donated green Volvo Gary had repaired and used to find parts and pick up small donations. Gary was allowed to use the rusty car outside his duties. It was surprising what people would throw out. A TV, microwave, and other unusual items Gary picked up then brought to his room. It wasn't stealing. It was borrowing.

He ended up here because he had been telling Gary Junior about his childhood and imparting God's Word since his son could understand right from wrong. He stopped recently when he finally saw how upset Junior became after each retelling of Troop injustices. He didn't know if his son's attitude was from embarrassment, pity, or rage. After the last childhood cathartic, Junior left the room in a fitful anger. That particular time was a revelation day. Gary realized how harmful these stories had been to Junior. He left the house in Meyersville that had once been a source of grief and pain, not wanting his son to endure the same. In the only altruistic act of his life, he spared Gary Junior from hearing more of his long-time woes and never looked back.

He was now ashamed that Gary Junior knew how he was picked on and treated by the Troop.

He should have kept his mouth shut about his youth, but these dark memories had to leak out. Like a pressure cooker, he had to expel steam now and then or go crazy.

He had to tell someone for release. Now, he had no one to vent to or pass on the word of the Lord.

Gary decided to pay a visit to the remaining Troop members just to see how scared they were and if any were ready to repent. He backed the Volvo out of the bay into the bright sun of midday and turned right onto Spring Street. Traveling through the Great Swamp brought back memories—not all bad. The good ones didn't involve the Troop. On Meyersville Road the worst memories did surface. Gary's old house was up the road from Steve's and, for a few fleeting moments, he was tempted to visit his son, but he turned into Steve's driveway. The gray house with a dual concrete arch supporting the second story porch loomed out of the hillside. Gary parked in the turnaround.

Steve and his family were having a quiet brunch in the kitchen when the doorbell chimed.

"Who could that be?" Steve's wife, Bethany, asked.

"I don't know. You and the children stay here."

Steve opened the door a crack, keeping the metal chain lock secure and tight. He was greeted by Gary as if the years hadn't rolled by.

"Hey, what's up?"

"Gary!"

"Yes, sir, in the flesh. How have you been?"

"Fine, fine, please come in." Steve slipped the chain lock free after giving Gary a look over for any visible weapons. "Dear, I'll be in the living room with a friend," he called to the kitchen. He didn't want his wife to meet Gary and he wanted Gray to know that there was someone else in the house.

After directing Gary to the couch, Steve started the conversation. "As a matter of fact, I've been looking for you."

"Well, here I am."

"Have you heard of the murders here?"

"Sure, I've been following them. They're the talk of the town."

"Oh?"

Gary pulled out a folded *Morristown Daily Record* newspaper from his back pocket and handed it to Steve. The folds were formed to present an article about the Long Hill Township murders.

Steve read the article, wincing at the title, realizing that he no longer had the leadership in this story and also recognizing how out of touch he had been. He expected the multiple murders to eventually catch the eye of other reporters, but not so soon. It seemed the Long Hill Police Department was more forthcoming with the *Daily Record* than the *Sentinel*.

MURDER MOST FOUL IN
LONG HILL TOWNSHIP
By Edwin Locker

A cluster of murders is centered in Long

Hill Township, west of Morristown. Four residents were brutally killed:

Kenneth Richardson, former Millington Boy Scout and Township inhabitant, was run over in New York City in broad day light. Witnesses say it was intentional. The driver was never caught.

Clancy Dickerson, another former Millington Boy Scout and Township resident, was pushed into the Millington Gorge and drowned. Tim Hardy, owner of Hardy's Repair, confessed to killing Mr. Dickerson to gain possession of a Lincoln Model L automobile. This case was solved due to the speedy and professional work of the Township's Police.

Paul Moody was shot in the head while attending the Chester Flea market. Not coincidentally, Mr. Moody was also a former Scout and lived with Peter Weber in Millington.

The next victim was Jack Calhoun who was strangled. Mr. Calhoun was the Scout Master of the same Millington Troop and, once again, a long-time resident of the Township. His murderer is still at large.

Could this be the work of a serial killer? Township Police think so. Lieutenant James Arnold informed this reporter of the investigation's progress. Suspects were narrowed down to people who knew the victims. The majority of Long

Hill Township residents are safe, but if you knew or had business with any of the deceased, please contact the Township Police as you may be danger.

The police department has hired auxiliary officers to patrol and assure locals a show of support for their safety. After a brief emergency training period, these new members will begin their duties within a week.

The police have also been monitoring the remaining Troop survivors both day and night.

In a related story, Mr. Donald Gold of Gillette fatally shot an office worker who was inquiring about his health since Gold had not shown up for work. Apparently, Mr. Gold thought the visitor was the serial killer. Police quickly arrived at the scene. Gold came out on the porch waving a 45 semi-automatic pistol. Thinking he meant harm, police shot Mr. Gold who expired at Morristown Memorial.

Lieutenant Arnold stated the local newspaper, the Echoes-Sentinel, *had placed an irrational fear in residents regarding the spat of killings.*

Steve crumpled the paper after reading the line about the *Echoes-Sentinel monitoring the remaining Troop survivors both day and night.*

"I haven't seen anyone nearby."

Gary was pleased to see his reaction. "The *Record* is doing a better job than you Steve."

Steve ignored the remark. "So what brings you here? You know, I've been looking for you."

"Really?"

"Yes, I wanted your take on the Troop murders."

"Well, Steve, old friend, that's exactly why I came to see you."

"Oh! Well, what do you think?"

"The Lord is avenging past wrongs."

Steve didn't expect this answer and didn't know how to address it. So he stumbled with, "Oh?"

"Yes, the Lord God Almighty is taking retribution for all the evil the Troop inflicted on some of its members and the church."

"Evil?"

"Yes, blatant evil. Do you remember Russell Baker, Samuel Voles, Teddy Nestor, or Giovanni Baglio?"

"Baker and Voles now live in another state. I know Teddy. I don't remember Baglio."

"Your clique tormented these boys."

"Clique? Tormented?"

"Yes, You, Richardson, Dickerson, Moody, and Weber persecuted those boys because they weren't like you.

"I don't know what you mean."

"Don't be stupid. I'm giving you the reason a serial killer would target the old Troop."

"We were just boys having fun. If we insulted or used anyone, we didn't mean it."

"It doesn't matter if you meant it or not. It was done. 'Proverbs 14:14: You harvest what you plant, whether good or bad.' You better look over your shoulder, Steve, you may be next." Gary abruptly rose and gave a stare toward the kitchen before he left the house.

Bethany heard the front door slam. "Who was that dear?"

"An old acquaintance came to visit. Nothing more." Unsettled, Steve sat at the kitchen table staring at a half-eaten cold tuna melt sandwich and pondering what had just happened: Was Gary admitting to being the serial killer? Could he be a copycat murderer? Steve began to feel fear being born.

Bethany stared at Steve and became concerned. She had known him since college and understood the look on his face. "PJ and Monique, you are excused from the table." The children hustled out to the television. Absently, Bethany her twirled shoulder-length auburn hair between her fingers before she asked, "What's the matter Steve?"

"Nothing."

"Was that about the murders of your friends?"

"No, no just work-related stuff."

Bethany recognized the set look on Steve's face, indicating the stubborn streak within. Once his mind was set, he pursued an ending, regardless of circumstances or outcome. "Steve—you're upset."

"Wilton accused the Troop of harassing other boys and maybe, maybe one of those boys is the killer."

"Who's Wilton?"

"An old time acquaintance. He was in the Troop for a while."

"Oh, well, I don't know. It seems a stretch to harbor a grudge all these years and then to act on it so violently. Did he say anything else?"

"No. You could be right."

"Certainly. He's not a reporter or with the police. Why would he know anymore?"

Bethany began to collect the dinner dishes. The conversation was uncomfortable. It felt good to get into a routine.

Steve retired to his desk in the bedroom. The fear hadn't gone away. It clung to him like light gauze.

❧❧❧

Smiling, Gary began the drive to Peter's house to spread the news of God's vengeance. He felt relieved, but not purged. The last time he was near this condition was his last conversation with Junior.

He was in luck. Peter was home and greeted him with the same quizzical look as Steve.

"Why do I deserve this visit?"

"I was just wondering how you've been holding up with the death of your partner and the others." Gary really wanted to say homo buddy instead of partner, but didn't want Peter to slam the door in his face. As he waited for Peter to reply, Gary remembered quotes from his Bible. Leviticus 18:22: "You shall not lie with a man as with a woman; it is an abomination." Leviticus 20:13: "If a man lies with a man as with a woman, both of them have committed an abomination; they shall be put to death, their blood is upon them."

Paul and Peter's had been a foul affair and Gary suspected the abomination started while they were in the evil Troop nest.

Peter stood in the doorway, not wanting this seedy, smelly man to enter. Gary didn't want to enter this den of iniquity, either. He shuddered at what had been going on behind that door: more reason for Paul to have died.

"What do you think of this whole thing, Peter?"

"What is the matter with you? I'm in deep grieving. I just don't want to think right now. I want to sit quietly and let all this flow past me."

"Okay, Peter. I hope you aren't next. Romans 1:18 'For the wrath of God is revealed from heaven against all ungodliness and unrighteousness of men, who by their unrighteousness suppress the truth.'"

The look on Peter's face was worth the trip.

Gary walked to his car for the drive to Teddy's house. This was a good day so far. He hadn't talked about the past with anyone for weeks. He felt the tension in his head discharging.

As he turned on Essex Street in Stirling, all the houses looked the same. He parked his car at the south end of Essex. He couldn't remember the number of Teddy's house so he stood in the middle of the street, cupped his hands around his mouth, and yelled to the north sky "Teddy!" No answer. Gray walked the street calling until a door opened.

"What's all the racket about?"

"I'm looking for Teddy Nester."

"Nester lives on the right. Number 19."

"Thank you." Gary returned to his car and drove half a block to the house.

Teddy still looked like a scarecrow, but a neater one. His hair was almost combed, shirt buttoned properly and his demeanor steady, "Gary. How are you doing?"

"Fine, just fine. Got me a new job repairing motors and such."

"That's great. Come in."

For these two, the years had made amends, and youthful animosity turned to friendship because of common experiences. Through the peeling screened porch into the house the two entered a small front room.

"Sit."

Gary sat on an old overstuffed plaid sofa and sank four inches into it. The room was almost bare. Just the sofa and another matching armchair occupied the modest space. White dingy walls accented the loneliness of the area. Teddy didn't entertain.

"What have you been doing lately, Teddy?"

"Still working at the Stirling Animal Hospital, feeding, cleaning up shit, washing cages, and the like. The hours are flexible and I like animals of all kinds, so it's good, good. What brings you here?"

"I've been around to see what is left of the old Troop."

"Why?"

"Just to see how they are taking the murders and put a little scare into them."

"Scare?"

"Yeah. It's nice to have the upper hand now."

"Who do you think is doing it?"

"You, me, or any of the other Scouts who suffered humiliation."

"That could be a big list."

"You know, a time is coming when all the bullies will be revenged. Firearms are easy to get, no background checks or anything. I can imagine kids mowing these bastards down and anyone who disrespected them."

"Kids can't buy weapons."

"But their parents can. Collections, hunting, sport shooting, street buying—there are millions of loose guns in households. I bought Gary Junior a .22 rifle with a 3 to 9X scope for plinking rats in the junk yard. Hell, you can even get a pistol off the Green in Morristown. As long as the NRA is around, weapons are easy to get. Thank you second amendment!"

"So you think a kid did this?"

"No, no, not these murders, I'm talking about the future. Kids will be shooting kids, mark my words. Bullying was and is common in schools. The teachers and administrators do nothing, nothing! The jocks and smart kids get all the attention. But the Troop killings required thought and planning, something a kid couldn't do."

"So who do think did it?

"I told you. Someone who was picked on by these guys. And he doesn't have to be a part of the Troop—maybe someone who was punched in the school hallway or was put down elsewhere."

"So you don't know."

Gary didn't answer.

"Don't you think the cops are investigating acquaintances and friends?" Teddy asked. "Even Troop members?"

"They don't know what they are doing. They came to visit me and got zero. The killer is far smarter than the police, despite what they say," Gary said with a smile. "Let's go see Johnny and get his take on this."

They walked up Main Avenue to the back of the Stirling Inn and into the kitchen.

"Johnny, you there?"

Giovanni came out of the food locker and greeted his visitors with enthusiasm. "What brings you here?"

"We wanted your thoughts on the recent killings."

"My thoughts?"

"Yes, who do you think did it?"

"Let's go outside."

The three sat on empty beer kegs. Giovanni lit an unfiltered cigarette and leaned forward as if he was revealing a secret. "I think one of us did it." He stared at the ground.

"Why do you think that?" Teddy asked, not surprised by the statement.

"Who else had a better reason?"

"But why after all these years?"

"Who knows? Maybe it took that long for the anger to rise."

Teddy frowned. "It's true that none of us had a reliable alibi for the days of the murders, but that doesn't make us valid suspects, Johnny."

"Look around you. I can swear that the cops have been watching the Hotel, watching me."

Teddy and Gary looked at each other, unaware that either had been under surveillance.

"It might be your imagination, Johnny," Teddy said. "I don't recall anyone following me."

"Me, neither," Gary agreed.

"The cops are not that obvious. They don't sit in cars eating donuts waiting for you to do something. They ask neighbors and employers to report on your whereabouts."

"How do you know this for sure?"

"I spent time in prison and learned a lot."

"Well, whoever is doing it, is a hero in my eyes," Gary put forth.

Giovanni and Teddy nodded.

cↄↄↄ

Steve approached Desk Sergeant Studnicky. "I'd like to see Lieutenant Arnold."

"Just a minute." The sergeant disappeared down a hall. In a few minutes he came back and motioned for Steve to step forward.

Steve followed him to a small office on the right.

Without a greeting, Steve asked, "What's this all about?" He placed the wrinkled *Daily Record* on the lieutenant's desk.

Arnold gave Steve a hard stare before picking up the article and perusing it. "What of it?"

"You gave more information to the *Record* than the *Sentinel*."

"So?"

"Don't you think your hometown paper deserves the same or more?"

"No, not with the inflammatory crap you are writing about the murders and the disrespect you are giving to your hometown police department."

"I write the truth!"

"You write what you want to, regardless of the truth. You know, I told you that you're to blame for the deaths of Gold and Neuman. I'm not the only one that thinks that."

"And I told you, you're crazy. I'm not responsible for all the quacks that are out there."

"You do have influence and this is why we aren't cooperating with you. You are dangerous."

"Dangerous?"

"Yes, sir, and by the way, you are also a suspect in these murders. Perhaps you are using the newspaper to distract us from yourself."

"This is preposterous and libelous. I will not stand for this treatment."

"How does it feel to be bullied, Mr. Mazur?"

"What?" Confused with the verbal attacks from Arnold, Steve was speechless and did what countless victims resorted to—he retreated.

Outside the police department, Steve stopped to gain control. What had just happened? His source of important information was cut off. He was not only accused of being a bad reporter, but was on a list of suspects for the serial killings. Where did he slip up?

He went back to the newspaper office to think things out.

It was very late and dark by the time Steve started home. He drove automatically, still trying to make sense of the conversation with Arnold. He found himself on Pond Hill Road, which was now paved. Lane lines were absent. Crossing guards were in place by the railroad tracks, but the edge of the Gorge still didn't have guard rails. While a few housing developments studded the right side away from the Gorge, it was still a lonely night drive to Valley Road, reminiscent of his mother's time.

Steve was tired from working so long the night before and today's confrontation had him thinking in circles. He slipped into a puzzle of thoughts lapsing again and driving on unconscious reflexes, aware only of the steep incline on his left as Gary's face appeared followed by Clancy's, terror in their eyes as they slipped faster and faster down in the river—the past and present becoming one.

The last couple of months were not as planned. His career was now in doubt and his friends were dead. This was not the future he had envisioned.

The deserted road was straight, smooth, and dark without street lamps. Steve drove through the night tunnel, following the cones of light spread before him. All the traffic was in the morning and afternoon when commuters hurried to the Millington Station to take the train to New York City.

In a driver's trance, he saw a shadow-mass dimly lit yards ahead just at the edge of the lights on the right side of road moving to the Gorge and toward him. He swerved to the left to avoid colliding with it. The car skidded and went over the edge, sliding on an angle over a carpet of loose leaves till the left front hit a large oak. The back end of the car kept moving and turning the entire vehicle vertical to the river before descending backward a few more feet till its left rear tire met a rock cropping and the fall stopped. The crash had thrown Steve into the expanding air bag, temporarily knocking him out. He was brought back to consciousness by a loud constant blare. His arm was trapped between the bag and the horn button on the steering wheel. His knees were pushed into his stomach. Pain had not yet made an appearance.

After a struggle, Steve managed to extradite his arm, open the car door, and wrench his legs free and, in the process, rolled ten more feet down before saplings halted his progress.

After resting for a good ten minutes, Steve crawled up the slope, aided by the one still glowing headlight. Upon reaching the road, he assessed himself for any major injuries. Pain, however, started to invade his nerves and take command. Fishing in his pocket, he managed to retrieve his cell phone and called 911 before passing out again.

At the hospital, he was pronounced sound though bruised. The attending doctor wanted to keep him overnight for observation, but Steve signed a waiver and was released. Upon notification from the hospital, Bethany had quickly arrived wearing pajamas and a terrycloth robe. She drove him home, fretting all the way about his poor driving. Steve told her he fell asleep at the wheel. No sense in alarming her.

Harding's Repair took three hours to haul up Steve's

car. It was parked to await the insurance inspector by the garage near a bay door that was still closed and locked.

In the afternoon, wearing a neck brace, more for show than damage, Steve returned to the Township Police Station and marched down the hall, Studnicky following in protest.

"Someone tried to kill me last night," he exclaimed to Lieutenant Arnold.

"I've just read the preliminary report. Seems you imagined something in the roadway."

"It wasn't something. It was someone who made me veer to the left and go over the edge, finally hitting a tree. It was deliberate."

"So you say."

"What do you mean?"

"We didn't find evidence of anyone being in the vicinity near your accident, but we did find deer prints alongside the road."

"It wasn't an accident. It wasn't a deer. It was the serial killer out to get me!"

"Mr. Mazur, you were tired. You admitted this yourself to the first responder. In semi-sleep a lot of shadows can appear and your imagination can provoke almost anything."

"I tell you he was real!"

"Possibly you concocted this story to move suspicion away from you."

"There you go again. What is the matter with you? What have you got against me?"

"I have nothing against you, Mr. Mazur. I'm just seeking the truth like you."

With that, Steve once again retreated from the office, knowing he wasn't convincing the lieutenant whose mind was set and immovable.

At the *Sentinel* everyone greeted him with sympathy. Gossip traveled fast.

Steve sat down to write another article. This one would be personal as well as factual about the lack of success the police were having in the so-called investigation of the serial killer.

The managing editor stepped up to Steve's desk. "What are you writing?"

"A follow up to the serial killer."

"No you're not."

Steve looked from his monitor. "What do you mean?"

"The police are complaining about your attitude and it hasn't yet been proven to be serial killings."

"You're going to be influenced by the police?"

"I'm going by editorial standards and what's good for the community. I'd rather you return to social news."

"Did you see the *Record's* account?"

"Yes I did and it was well-rounded."

"You can't be serious!"

"I am. We will not print any more articles about this

until we have valid information, not speculation. It has been weeks since the last murder. Lay this thing to rest. The Township residents can only take so much. You have been more a disruption than the murders."

"I was almost killed last night."

"You were tired and ran off the road. I want you to take the rest of the week off and recuperate fully."

"But—"

"Enough, Steve. Write a social column or go home."

❦❦❦

I've been silent too long. The end is near. I must decisively act soon to continue my mission and it must be big. The police are nowhere near to discovering me and I will keep it that way with my brilliant plan by focusing their attention. This time it will be big, big!

❦❦❦

Gary Wilton Junior called Teddy, visited Giovanni, and left a note at the Salvation Army for his father, inviting them to a get together at ten Saturday morning. He asked his neighbor, Ricky Kubick as well. Beer in the refrigerator, chips, dips, and pizza ought to keep all at the house for a while. Ricky was the first to arrive, followed by Giovanni and Teddy. Junior made introductions and brought out the beer.

"What's the occasion?" asked Teddy.

"Nothing special, just a get together. I thought you all haven't seen each other for a while and I haven't seen Ricky in a long time, even though we're neighbors."

"Oh we've been in touch especially since these Troop killings."

"Yeah it's a shame." Gary tried to sound sincere and went to answer a timid knock on the front door.

Gary Senior stood mute, head down.

"Dad! Great to see you!"

"Really? I didn't know you wanted to see me again after all the complaining and grief I gave you about my childhood."

"Nonsense. Things are working out."

Junior made sure the conversion was flowing before he silently left the house through a back door.

eↄeↄ

Peter Weber almost couldn't get out of bed that morning. Everything in the house reminded him of Paul. Every room was filled with antiques and the presence of Paul. It was becoming insufferable to remain here, but unthinkable to leave all these memories. He had to make a decision though. Each day didn't get any better. He knew Paul would want him to move forward. Perhaps not only leaving the house, but locating outside Long Hill Township would be beneficial, maybe nearer the hospital.

Placing one foot at a time on the carpet, Peter eased upright and headed for the bathroom. The mirror magnified the misery he had been coping with.

Morristown Memorial had called. He had a hard time understanding the muffled voice, but attributed this to his malaise. Apparently, the chief of staff wanted him in at eleven-thirty today. Though he didn't feel like going, it was a step toward normalcy.

Paul finished washing and dressed in his best suit, hoping it might camouflage his current demeanor.

He drove to the center of Morristown and made a right on South Street to Madison Avenue and the hospital.

As he parked, he saw an object arc over the cars on his right. It shattered on his car roof and exploded.

ผวผ

Steve tried to rest, but his dreams didn't allow it.

He had received an odd muffled call with a short message last night: Gary Wilton was ready to talk to him and him only at eleven-thirty in the morning about the killings. He was to meet Gary at the Morristown Green on the corner of East Park Place and South Park Place. Based on what Gary had said, Steve believed him to be the killer, but without solid evidence he had nothing to go on. He should call the police or even his paper, but if he was wrong, his creditability would really tumble.

"Bethany, I'll be gone for a while," he called into the house as he stepped onto the front porch. He almost fell over a five pound container of fertilizer. Material leaked from a split in the bag bottom when he picked it up. Cursing, Steve placed his hand over the tear to stop the outflow and brought it to the back shed. Bethany must have been feeding the pansies around the porch stairs. He'd have to talk with her about leaving stuff in traffic areas.

Steve managed to find metered parking on Washington Street. He was on the opposite corner of the Green. He glanced at his watch: 11:15. He would be on time. Crossing North Park Place, he headed to the corner meeting spot. This could be the conclusion to a great story and, more importantly, the end of his inward fear of the killer.

The Morristown Green dated back to 1715 and was one of only two greens in New Jersey to have survived to the present day. It was a focal point of the town, hosting political and cultural events throughout the year.

The Green was an irregular square of two and a half acres of grass, flowers, ornamental plants, statues, historic plaques, walk ways, a fountain, and benches surrounded by a Presbyterian and United Methodist church, restaurants, banks, and other businesses. It was an encampment for George Washington and the Continental Army in 1777 after victories at Trenton and Princeton. It was used as a public executions ground, the last execution taking place in 1833.

Gary wasn't at the corner location, so Steve sat on a park bench and waited. It was a pleasant morning with ample sunshine. People hurried along concrete walkways on the edge of the Green, ignoring the flowers and the contentment of a natural environment so easily within reach. Steve was relaxed, certain his meeting with Gary would end the events of the past months. He would be justified in his concern and actions. Gary was either the serial killer or knew who was. He would have a scoop and beat the *Daily Record*. Steve's peace of mind was about to be shattered.

As he looked at his watch again, a very loud report issued from the south. Construction?

Minutes later, the wailing of police sirens filled the air. Something had happened.

Everyone in the park and on the sidewalks stopped to listen and stare in the direction of the hospital where smoke arose.

Steve was torn between investigating the cause of the blast and smoke or waiting a little longer. After twenty-five minutes, without the appearance of Gary, he started to walk toward the smoke in the distance. A crowd had gathered on Morris Street. Police prevented anyone from going further.

"I'm Steve Mazur, a reporter for the *Echoes-Sentinel* in Long Hill Township."

"I don't care who you are. No one gets past this point."

"What happened?"

"All I know is there was an explosion at the hospital."

"Anyone killed?"

"I don't know anything else. Please step back."

All the streets to the south of the Green were being cordoned off. Traffic was at a standstill and bottled up on the other side of the park as well.

Since it was obvious that Gray wasn't going to show, Steve walked back to Washington Street.

When Steve reached Bethany's car, the door was slightly ajar—hardly enough to notice, but Steve was wary of everything now. Nothing seemed missing, though he really didn't know what his wife kept in the glove compartment or on the back seats. He probably didn't close it all the way in his rush to meet Gary.

Steve could envision a conspiracy in everything except his personal life. He viewed himself as a reporter outside events. This attitude would ultimately be his downfall.

With building traffic congestion, it took Steve an hour to leave the town and return home. He called the office, but no one was aware of an explosion in Morristown.

It was probably sewer gas or a car crash. It could wait till morning. He would also search for Gary then.

୧୬୧୬

Late the next morning the doorbell awoke Steve from a needed deep sleep on the sofa after Bethany, PJ, and Monique went shopping. He answered the call, but before he could open the door, he heard an authoritarian voice.

"This is Lieutenant James Arnold from the Long Hill Police Department with two officers. Please open the door."

As the door swung open, the Lieutenant handed Steve a paper, "This is a search warrant for your house, out buildings, yard, and automobiles."

"Search warrant?"

"Yes. Please step aside so we can proceed."

"I don't understand."

"We have reasonable suspicion that you were involved in yesterday's bombing."

"Bombing?"

"Playing innocent will not get you anywhere, Mr. Mazur. Please remove yourself from the doorway and step to the right."

Steve backed off. One of the officers frisked him while the lieutenant and other officer searched the living room. Steve started to follow.

"Stay where you are, Mr. Mazur. I don't want to handcuff you."

"The explosion was a bomb?"

No one answered.

It took two hours for a complete examination of the

entire house. The search then went outside to the shed and yard.

Arnold came back into the house. "Did you get a replacement car yet?"

"No, my car is at Hardy's Repair in Millington waiting on insurance inspection."

"Do you own another?"

"Yes, my wife is using it now. Listen, I don't know what you are doing here—"

"Where were you yesterday around eleven-thirty yesterday?"

"I was in Morristown at the Green."

"On business?"

"Yes, you might call it that."

"Well, what was it?"

"I was on an investigation and I don't have to reveal anything."

"Exactly where is your wife?"

"She's with my kids at The Valley Mall Shopping Center."

"Please give this officer the license plate number, make, and color of the car."

"No, I don't want her or the children involved in whatever this is."

"Make it easy on everyone, especially your family."

After consulting an address book in an end table nearby, Steve gave the policeman the number, color, and make of the car.

"Okay, I'm asking you to voluntarily come with us to the station. Officers will drive your wife home."

"Why?"

"You need to explain some things. Is this the same shirt you wore yesterday?"

"No, it's in the upstairs hamper. May I leave a note for my wife?"

"Officer, retrieve all the shirts in the hamper and clothes closet. You will be allowed two phone calls at the station, Mr. Mazur. Don't be confrontational. I don't want to have to restrain you. We have probable cause and an arrest warrant. You don't want to make your situation worse"

"Confrontational? I believe you're biased, Lieutenant."

"Just doing a thorough investigation, Mr. Mazur. Just doing my job."

"So this is an arrest."

"Yes, sir, it is. You are a prime suspect in the recent attempted murder. I'm taking you in for questioning."

"Murder? Who? When?"

He was read the Miranda Rights: "You have the right to remain silent and to refuse to answer questions. Anything you do say may be used against you in a court of law. You have the right to consult an attorney before speaking to the police and to have an attorney present during questioning now or in the future. If you cannot afford an attorney, one will be appointed for you before any questioning if you wish. If you decide to answer questions now without an attorney present, you will still have the right to stop answering at any time until you talk to an attorney."

An officer finished reading the laminated card, grabbed Steve's arm, and walked toward the door.

"Wait, wait." Steve scribbled a short note, hoping to calm Bethany when she came home in police custody, and placed it on the end table.

He rode in the back of a police car. None of his questions were answered. He was booked and taken to a small interrogation room.

Steve refused to contact an attorney, thinking this would be tantamount to admitting any guilt.

Three hours had passed since a technician came and scraped his finger nails and swabbed his hands. It was quiet. This room was just like the ones on the television shows he and Bethany watched. Spartan, cold, and empty except for a bare table with two folding chairs. Steve looked at his reflection in the mirrored glass on the opposite wall. He didn't like what he saw. He actually looked scared and this could be construed as a guilty look.

The lieutenant reentered the room and slapped a folder on the table before Steve. "Preliminary reports indicate the bomb was made with potassium permanganate. We found an open bag of it in your shed. Furthermore, trace elements were discovered on your hands and shirt."

"I don't know how to make a bomb."

"Anyone can find bomb instructions using the internet. This particular one was in a glass container, like the jelly jar we saw in your refrigerator. Coat the inside of the jar with gasoline; add a few drops of water to the potassium permanganate, and it's ready. This fertilizer is easily obtainable from Lowes. The bomb was so simple an eighth grader could do it. All you have to do is throw it against something hard. Depending on the size of the glass container and amount of fertilizer used, it could have the power of a half stick of dynamite!"

"This is ridiculous!"

"The Morristown Police confirmed that you were seen near the hospital. This all begins to add up, Mr. Mazur."

"I moved a bag of fertilizer from the front porch. I thought my wife was feeding the flowers, and I was blocks away from the explosion, anyway."

"No sign of this fertilizer type was discovered on your lawn or shrubs. The Green is within walking distance from the hospital. Furthermore, we found a prepaid phone, also known as a burner, under the front seat of your wife's car—the same car you used that day. The records show that the only calls made were to you and Paul Weber on this same phone near your house. Obviously you called yourself to establish an alibi. You rubbed your fingerprints off but you should have thrown the phone away. "

"Wait a minute, Paul Weber was the victim?"

"It appears he was the target of the bomb."

"Is he all right?"

"He's in intensive care."

"Listen, I received a phone call and was told to meet Gary Wilton on the Green. He had something to tell me. I believe him to be the killer."

"This morning the Morristown Police checked with Mr. Wilton. He did not call you. In fact he doesn't own a phone and he has a rock solid alibi."

"I found the car door ajar after my failed meeting. Someone must have placed the phone there. Don't you see? This is the work of the serial killer and he's trying to frame me!"

"Yes, for once I agree with you about a serial killer and based on your fabricated stories and past actions and with the evidence we just collected, I believe you are that serial killer."

"Maybe I need a lawyer."

"Yes, I believe you do, Mr. Mazur. I'm detaining you for the attempted murder of Peter Weber. You will be kept overnight."

Steve was ordered to empty his pockets. His personal property and money was inventoried and placed in the station's safe.

He was finally allowed two phone calls: to Bethany and his lawyer.

"Honey, I'm at the police station. They want to keep me overnight on suspicion of trying to kill Peter Weber."

"*What*? That's crazy!"

"I know, I know, it's ridiculous, but there is nothing I can do now.

"I'll come right down."

"No, no don't come down. I'm going to call Jonathan and he'll get a writ of habeas corpus so I can be brought before a judge to determine if I'm lawfully held. I'll keep you informed. Stay home for the kids. Please call the *Sentinel* and let them know of this situation."

"I will. I love you."

"I love you too."

Steve's next and final call was to Jonathan Crisptan of Crisptan and Morgan. He explained his situation and Jonathan agreed to handle it.

The next day, Steve and Jonathan appeared before the judge. Noting the seriousness of the offense charged and based on the police request for a longer holding time, the judge ordered Stephen to remain in jail for another four days as the investigation continued.

എഹെഹ

Gary Senior was in a good mood till he reached the outskirts of Morristown. The traffic was backed-up, but he used this waiting time to reflect on the morning, instead of becoming his usual angry self. His son had actually invited him over and appeared to have forgiven him for all the excuses, grief, and pain he had burdened Junior with these last couple of years. God was smiling. The conversation was interesting and he enjoyed the company. Junior had disappeared, but came back with sandwiches from the Myersville Café for a late lunch. Gary guessed that Junior just wanted the conversation of old men to be unimpeded by a younger person's presence. It didn't matter.

This was the start of something good.

After an hour of slow movement, Gary arrived at the Salvation Army to be met by two Morristown Police officers who questioned him about his morning. Gary asked what it was about, but received no information. After thirty minutes of queries, the officers left.

Gary returned to his car and drove to see Teddy. As he turned onto Essex Street, a patrol car backed out of Teddy's driveway. Gary pulled to the side and waited till it had turned on Main Avenue before parking in front of the house.

Teddy was still standing on the front porch steps as Gary approached.

"What was that about?"

"They asked me about my activities this morning," Teddy replied.

"I was questioned too. Do you know what happened?"

"Yeah, they said a bomb was exploded at Morristown Memorial and Peter Weber was hurt."

"Weber! Hurt or dead?"

"Still alive in intensive care. A lot of facial burns and glass fragments."

"Almost the last to go. That just leaves Mazur of the originals."

"Well, he's not dead yet. Do you suppose we will be next? What if this is just a crazed person selecting at random a group of people, like Troop 186, for no real reason? That means me, you, and Johnny and other others associated with the Troop are targets as well." Teddy started to get jittery. Once again his arms began to flail. The Troop murders weren't satisfying now if he was to be a target too.

"Well, I thought it might be one of us, but we were all together this morning."

"I'm worried now, Gary. I'd rather be a spectator than a participant. Maybe one of us outcasts is really next."

"Take it easy, Teddy. Despite what Mazur says, it may not be a serial killer but just a lot of coincidences. I don't think we have anything to worry about. We're still the invisible people. Others don't care or choose to ignore us as usual."

Teddy started to walk in circles, hoping kinetic energy would relieve the tension and anxiety now building inside of him. He was regressing. All the traits of his youth would soon start to show. All the medicine and restraint over the last years were escaping at this very moment.

Gary tried to comfort Teddy—something he was ill suited to do. Tentatively, he patted a shoulder and uttered low soothing phrases. "Don't be upset, we really don't know anything. It's all right, Teddy, just relax." He managed to sit Teddy on the sofa and went into the kitchen to get some tea.

The kitchen wasn't used to occupants. Most of the cupboards were empty. The refrigerator barely contained edible food. Thick paint strips were shedding from the bare walls. The echo of his steps on the linoleum floor exaggerated the emptiness of the stark white room. Though his living conditions were not much better, arguably worse, this room, this house were shadow ghosts of the living. Gary had never felt so sorry for Teddy until now.

Finding dried tea bags, Gary started to boil water in a pot. He didn't bother to look for sugar and there wasn't milk in the refrigerator. He was lucky to find a tea cup.

"Here you go, Teddy. This will be calming."

Teddy had either passed out or was sleeping sitting up. Gary placed the tea on a blue painted coffee table. There was nothing more he could do. He left, congratulating himself on his care for Teddy.

Something was clouding his thoughts as he started the car, a question he didn't want to recognize and subconsciously fought against all late morning—the reason Junior had disappeared and where he actually went. The Myersville Café wasn't that far away.

സ്ക

The second floor intensive care unit was white and sterile. Low sounds of life extending machines and occasional whispers of doctors, nurses, and attendants fought against the quiet and serious environment. An endotracheal tube was inserted into Weber's trachea to provide air to his lungs. A cardiac monitor kept track of life signs. A web of intravenous fluids, containing a feeding tube, electrolytes, antibiotics, and blood transfusion lines hung above his head.

Peter was propped into a sitting position to elevate his head and arms above his heart. Third degree burns scarred his head, face, and arms. His right eye had been punctured by a glass shard. Sterile bandages were wrapped like a mummy to protect what was now his skin: black, white, and yellow dead tissue. Sedatives kept him at rest. For the first time in weeks, Peter did not think about Paul, did not think at all.

A police officer stood bored outside the room as a precaution. He visibly became rigid as Lieutenant Arnold approached.

"Everything all right?"

"Yes, sir."

"Anyone come to visit?"

"No one besides medical."

"He awake?"

"It wouldn't matter if he was. There are so many

tubes in him and in his mouth. His face is covered with gauze."

"Okay." Arnold entered the room.

Weber was motionless. He looked like a cocoon or a corpse being regenerated in a science fiction tale, but he was alive. Arnold needed to see the attending doctor to find out when he could question him. It didn't look like soon.

Out in the hall, he looked for a doctor and, not seeing any, went to the nurse's station and inquired who Weber's assigned doctor was.

"And are you a relative?"

The lieutenant was wearing his civilian clothes as he always did on investigations. It was less intimating than a brass uniform.

Arnold presented his badge to the nurse. "No, I'm Lieutenant James Arnold investigating Mr. Weber's attempted murder."

The nurse reached for the patient's folder and skimmed it, "That would be Dr. Roger Enfield."

"And where would he be?"

"Perhaps on rounds or in the doctor's lounge."

"Which way to the lounge?"

"Down this hall and turn right. The door is locked. You will have to knock."

"Thank you."

Arnold knocked and, in a few seconds, the door was opened.

"Is Doctor Enfield here?"

"No, he's on ward six. Up one flight of stairs or take the elevator."

"Thank you."

The lieutenant found Enfield outside a room talking to three interns. He waited till the conversation was over.

"Doctor Enfield, I'm Lieutenant James Arnold from the Long Hill Police Department. I need to know when Peter Weber will be conscious. I need to ask him questions about the bombing."

"We are transferring him to The Burn Center at Saint Barnabas in Livingston. We can't handle Dr. Weber's condition. Saint Barnabas is the only state-certified burn treatment facility in New Jersey and one of the largest in North America.

"When would this be?"

"When he has been stabilized and as soon as a bed at the Center opens. Most likely the day after tomorrow."

"Thank you."

Arnold returned to the Long Hill Police Department. Announcing to the room at large: "Do any of you have connections in Livingston?"

"Why, Lieutenant?"

"Weber is being transferred to Saint Barnabas in two days. I was unable to question him. I need to know when he will be ready to talk."

"I have a buddy from the Academy in the Livingston Department."

"Good, Molosic. Contact him right away. I want to know the minute Weber is awake. I want to nail Mazur to the cross and end all of this. And, Sergeant, since you are still on desk assignment, I want you to escort the ambulance. I'll let you know time and route."

e⁄ɔe⁄ɔ

Gary Junior was glad his father came over. It was the start to making amends and, when his father knew what he had done, it would not only make his father proud, but stop the turmoil Gary Senior had bottled up for so long and repeated so often.

Junior had read the latest *Daily Record* article by Edwin Locker. Mazur was suspected not only of the attempted murder of Weber, but of all the other Township resident killings, except for Dickerson. Locker claimed that the Long Hill Police had evidence of the Morristown bombing associated with Mazur. His prior actions and the articles in the *Echoes-Sentinel* by Mazur were attempts to lure the police away from suspecting him. Besides his association with Troop 186, police were still searching for a pattern.

They knew that the average serial killer was a white male from a lower-to-middle-class background, usually in his twenties or thirties. They could be alcohol abusers. As children, fledgling serial killers often tortured animals. Neighborhood interviews and background checks seem to indicate these pertained to Mazur. Lieutenant Arnold was confident he had caught the serial killer.

Junior's plan had succeeded. By the grace of God, justice was nearly accomplished.

There were a few loose ends to clear up as soon as Mazur was released from jail. Weber was still alive and that was a problem. Gary hadn't decided on whether to kill Mazur or let him rot in jail. There was always the chance that he wouldn't be convicted, but killing him would mean an ongoing investigation and Junior's involvement might be revealed even though he had been careful.

Junior knew that he had actually liked the planning and execution: waiting till the right moment and then acting, eliminating life. It was especially satisfying when he could feel or see life fading away. No, not fading away but seeping into his being, feeding a vague yet real hunger. It was the power of powers! The danger that might occur with Mazur's demise energized him. The risk was less than the reward.

After these retributions were completed, Junior would tell his father, knowing his father would take satisfaction, even solace, in the deaths of these childhood bullies and even pride in who did it! But wait, Gary Senior might reveal Junior's work to Teddy and Johnny. So perhaps they should be next before he told Gary Senior. This would ensure silence and Junior's safety. By eliminating both, Junior could continue as a serial killer. But wait,

Junior wasn't not a serial killer. He was an avenger, a righteous righter of wrongs. And he was clever. Serial killers had a definite murder pattern. He was careful not to establish an obvious blueprint. Besides a distance association with Troop 186, his pattern was that there was no pattern. How clever! Yes, he wasn't a serial killer. He was a righteous judge. He had begun to rectify his father's past and would continue to eliminate all living reminders of it. And as a bonus, by removing one or more who of those who were actually bullied would also seem to get rid of the real motivation, though he doubted the police would ever be that intuitive or professional. Junior would save Mazur for the last. The anticipation was drug-like.

Junior needed to see Sergeant Molosic to gather needed information about Weber and Mazur through casual conversation. The sergeant believed his enthusiasm and abilities were always overlooked. Flattery contributed to his boasting and self-importance. Junior had frequently helped Molosic in illegal weapons purchases by crossing the state line to Pennsylvania and buying a trunk full of semi-automatic rifles, pistols, even a grenade launcher. Firearms weren't registered and state permits for long guns and handguns weren't required. The state didn't even have an assault weapons law and owner's licenses weren't requisite. Delaware had the same loose laws.

Junior leveraged this unlawful "partnership" with

Molosic to keep abreast of the police investigations into the serial murders. The sergeant was more than happy to relate that he was off desk duty and would ride escort for Weber.

Junior suspected the sergeant shot Gold to hide his involvement with Gold's stash of illegal weapons. This suspicion and his employment with Molosic gave Junior an advantage in the form of a silent comradeship the sergeant didn't experience within the department. This situation added to Junior's overall stimulation.

He began to shake with his own pomposity for having so much knowledge and power.

e*e*

Junior drank from the Jack Daniels bottle and took a Lithium—a ritual he started with Richardson's death. Uttering, "Harmful acts are always intentional," he headed to the junkyard.

Placing the bottle on an old tire rim, he searched for one of the few cars in running condition. Taking the ignition key from behind the visor, Junior started a 1956 Chrysler 300 amid a cloud of blue smoke emanating from the tail pipe.

If the car had been in mint condition, it would be worth up to one hundred thousand dollars, but corrosion on the front floor, trunk pans, and rocker panels, dented lower rear quarter panels, hand painted exterior, bad brakes, and a continuing list of needed repairs made the 300 a money pit. But it would serve his purpose.

He wore a Mets baseball cap with the brim over his eyebrows and pressed on a black moustache he found in a years-old Halloween box. His disguise was completed with a common hunter's camouflage jacket and matching pants. Latex gloves were in his pocket. He hoped he looked older than his twenty-two years.

With license plates recovered from another car and the vehicle identification number removed from the dashboard, engine block, car frame, rear wheel well, drive-side doorjamb, side post, and under the spare tire, he drove out of the junk yard, confident the car couldn't be traced. On the passenger seat, cradled in rags were two mayonnaise jars filled with the potassium permanganate solution.

Because of the previous informal conversation, Molosic had provided the route Weber would travel to Saint Barnabas: Columbia Turnpike which turned into South Orange Avenue, left on Walnut, left on Hillside then a right onto Park Drive. Gary decided that he would wait on Peach Tree Hill Road. It was fairly secluded and had a good view of the South Orange east bound traffic.

※※※

The Morristown Ambulance squad arrived promptly at the hospital nine in the morning to transport Peter to

Livingston nine miles away. Discharge and transfer papers were complete. Weber and the web of tubes and wires keeping him alive were rolled out on a gurney and pushed into the patient compartment.

The medical van eased into Madison Avenue. Sirens were not necessary since the patient was stabilized and unconscious. It would be a quick and uneventful ride.

Sergeant Molosic followed behind in an unmarked car, an open bag of donut holes beside him. The morning rush was about over so the roads were relatively clear. Molosic became comfortable and reported in that the trip had begun.

He reached into the bag and pulled out a glazed coconut hole, his favorite. He hoped by solving these murders, Arnold would be made chief and the lieutenant position would become open. He, naturally, would be the chose for promotion because of his abilities and the fact that the only other sergeant in the department was Studicky, who manned the desk and had no real field experience.

A few cars had squeezed into the safety zone between him and the ambulance. Normally this would call for a warning or a ticket, but he was out of his jurisdiction and couldn't stop anyway.

There wasn't a safe way to get directly in back of the medical van. The vehicles in front allowed more cars to cross into the fast lane, pushing Molosic farther back. He wasn't worried. The hospital was near.

ᴄ∕ᴐᴄ∕ᴐ

They crossed over the Passaic River, nearing Peach Tree Hill Road. Junior was ready. He gloved his hands and put the car in gear. As the ambulance passed by, he sped out into the second east bound lane and pulled alongside. Blindly reaching with his right hand, he grabbed a jar and hurled it out his driver window. The bomb hit the ambulance on the passenger window, shattering it and exploding. The force of the blast had caused both vehicles to swerve to the shoulder of each lane. The EMT became engulfed in flames. With arms waving in a frantic effort to smother the fire, he only spread the flames in a frenzied dance of death. The ambulance limped to a stop in a ditch. High-pitched screams emerged from the blazing cab, its occupant frantically trying to find the door handle in a blind panic. With each intake of air for the next agonizing yell, his throat and lungs seared.

Junior turned a hard left, tires screeching, leaving rubber on the pavement. The old car itself crying in pain. He came abreast of the smoking emergency vehicle and slid to a stop. Traffic had come to a standstill in the slow lane. Drivers were amazed and frightened at the burning inferno. No one came out of the safety of their cars to aid the ambulance's occupants. Racing out, running low because of the heat, Junior opened the passenger compartment door. The back was full of dark smoke. Weber was strapped in the tilted gurney unaware of his fate. The paramedic had fallen was lying against the side wall dazed. Gary stepped back and threw the remaining bomb under the gurney. It exploded sending the bed toward the ceiling. Satisfied, Gary turned around to see the line of cars before him. Bending his head down, he quickly returned to his car and sped off as a second more violent blast detonated oxygen tanks.

He chuckled, looking at the carnage through his rear view mirror. This task was finally completed.

᠁

The air conditioner and closed windows muffled the sound of the first explosion. Molosic only became aware of the situation when the cars in front abruptly came to a halt. His open bag of donuts fell and holes rolled all over the cruiser. He picked up a chocolate one near the automatic shifter and popped it into his mouth. Damn traffic. He rolled down the window as the second explosion occurred. He looked beyond the cars in front of him and saw a wall of smoke and flame. Was the ambulance on fire? Was this another attack on Weber! He hoped that Weber was all right for the sake of Molosic's career. Leaving the car, he moved quickly to the inferno. As he neared, he realized no one could survive the hot and pervasive blazing structure. Paint blistered and blackened. The scorching air smelled acrid with a faint odor of roasted pig. Molosic looked for a second vehicle that must be involved then ran back and called for help. This was not good, but he could salvage this if he started to interview the drivers ahead of him immediately. Ignoring the east bound traffic jam building every minute, he started with the drivers immediately in back of the flaming ambulance. His worse fear was realized. This was not an accident, but a murder. Drivers recounted a beat-up gray car, make and model unknown, with large back fins speeding past the wreckage, throwing something, and the driver then opening the back and tossing what appeared to be jar that exploded. No one knew what the third detonation was. Descriptions of the person ranged from short, dark with a moustache to a tramp with a Yankees baseball cap to a crazed hunter to an Islamic terrorist. License plate numbers ran the range of the alphabet and numeric system to not remembering at all.

This was bad. Not good at all for him. He now sat in the cruiser waiting for help, picking up the errant donut holes and ignoring the building traffic jam on the west bound side of South Orange Avenue as well. He didn't have an appetite now. This definitely was not good for his career. He played back the scenario. The sergeant seemed to remember a gray car speeding in the right lane approaching the ambulance. There was something about the driver he couldn't quite place.

eⱭeⱭ

Gary drove south to Howell Township where his friend, Jason Blewett, had a salvage yard with a car crusher. He had been selling Jason junk cars because of a recent ordinance requiring him to clean up the acres of old cars behind the house. This also gave him food and spending money, some of which he saved in a wall hole behind his bedroom dresser and in his secret hiding place out back.

"Jason, I have car for you to crush. I was on some errands and it started to act up so I thought I'd drop it off."

"Is this a 1956 Chrysler 300?"

"Yeah. Listen, if you could give me a lift home, you can have it for free." Gary didn't want any receipt that could be traced.

"Sure thing." Jason had no intention of crushing the car.

ↄ◌ↄ

Steve was lying on the steel bedstead facing the back green painted cinderblock wall of the six-by-eight foot cell, biting his fingernails. He was truly scared and confused now. The realization that he was a viable target was hitting home. He could be next, but at least the cell was a safe haven for now. He tried to make sense of the past events. The serial killer was someone close. Someone who knew the victims and their daily activities so he had to be from the Township. The killer was also someone who knew him, and probably had some sort of perverse connection to Troop 186. Steve still tried to convince himself he wasn't in danger. Clancy and Gold were not a part of this, but tied up to all the murders. Was Peter right? Could these be just a coincidence? And perhaps it was a deer that Steve encountered at the gorge, but he was the last troop member and there appeared no end in sight to these slayings. Surely, someone was after the Troop, but why? It couldn't be Gary as Steve had suspected—he had an alibi. Who would wait all these years to seek what? Vengeance? For what? Steve finally came to the realization that he was no longer a small town reporter looking for the big break. He was the next target since he was the last Troop member. This was very, very personal.

The barred door opened, disrupting his rambling thoughts.

"Get up, you're free to go."

"What?"

"Get up. You're free." The officer tossed a bag containing his personal items on the floor.

"What happened?"

"Peter Weber was killed yesterday with the same bomb type used before."

"Who did it?"

"We don't know yet. It is under investigation."

"Yeah, under investigation," Steve muttered.

"Pardon me?"

"Never mind."

The officer left. Steve rummaged through the bag and retrieved his items. He quickly changed out of the orange prison jumpsuit. The cell door remained open. Steve felt reluctant to leave, but his family was outside. Perhaps they were in danger as well. The others didn't have dependents. Steve walked out.

The desk sergeant motioned to him. "Mr. Mazur, please sign this form indicating all your things including money have been returned," he said in a monotone.

"Is Lieutenant Arnold in? I need to see him."

"No, he's out," was all that was offered.

Steve called a taxi and went home to convince Bethany to take the children and visit her parents out of state. She was unwilling to go at first, worried for her Steve, but finally relented and started packing.

Convinced of his family's safety, Steve took the waiting taxi to the office, carefully watching out the passenger windows for something, though exactly what he wasn't sure of. Everyone was startled to see him walk in. Some were apprehensive, some afraid. The managing editor motioned for him to come to his office where it was more private.

"What happened?"

"I was turned loose because the serial killer struck again. He finished Peter Weber with the same bomb he used initially. The jail was my alibi."

"Yes, I know. Here's an initial report."

"How did you get that?"

"When you're on good terms with the police, news and law go together. Remember that."

"Okay, I will. I'm going to write an update to the serial killer story."

"I think you need a rest, Steve. Say a couple of weeks."

"I don't need rest, I need to work."

"Steve, you were detained for murder, make that murders. Some in the office are afraid."

"They have nothing to be afraid of, you know that."

"I've known you for years, and yes, I'm not afraid. I don't think for one minute that you are capable of killing. I'm only thinking of others."

"I need to work. I need to find this killer. I need to write another article. I need to do something!"

"Okay. Write the article, let me approve it then go home for the day. And go easy on the police or the article won't make it past my desk."

"Sure."

VALLEY KILLER STILL AT LARGE
By Stephen Mazur

Long Hill Township: Peter Weber, an internist with the Morristown Memorial Hospital and long-time resident of the Township, was the latest target of the Valley Killer. Having failed after a bomb exploded at the Morristown Memorial parking lot, the killer finished his task by destroying the ambulance containing a comatose Weber on South Orange Avenue with the same type of explosive used in the previous attempt. Weber was being transported to the Saint Barnabas Burn Unit. EMT Robert Evan died of horrible burns when the homemade bomb was tossed into the cab by the Valley Killer as he drove by. Mr. Evan is survived by his wife and three-year-old daughter. Mr. Weber was torn apart by a second bomb tossed into the patient compartment of then disabled vehicle. The blast and subsequent flames finally ended Weber's life as well as Paramedic Dominic Ferrera who is survived by his parents. The killer escaped without pursuit in an old gray car with large tail fins. Witnesses were unable to agree on the perpetrator's description even though it was a clear day and the killer was not more than twenty feet away from the ambulance when he tossed the final bomb into the back.

At the time of the horrific event, this reporter had been incarcerated on suspicion of being the Valley Killer, despite the fact that an attempt on his life had occurred. My news coverage and opinions had eventually biased the police against me. The police must now return to square one and start the investigation again.

A failed Township Police escort was follow-ing the ambulance to ensure Mr. Weber's safety. This reporter is formally requesting protection as the last of Troop 186 and therefore the mostly likely next victim. How good this protection will be, based on the recent events is hard to tell.

This continued reign of terror needs to come to an end. Perhaps this is the time to call in the State Trooper Violent Crime Analysis Unit. Using computers and algorithms, this unit analyzes violent crimes through comparison of specifics such as date, location, modus operan-di, victimology, offender description, offender behavior, involved vehicles, and weapons. The Violent Crime Analysis Unit will facilitate coop-eration, communication, and coordination with our local police department and if need be, the FBI. It is clear that help is needed.

The Valley Killer is becoming self-assured and bold in this murderous rampage. Anyone with information: unusual behavior of neighbors or friends, previous connections with any Scout Troop member, notice of an old gray car, any-thing—please contact me at smazur@msn.com or the police.

Steve was satisfied that this small article would galvanize the police department into action. He was thoroughly fearful that his life was in serious danger. He brought the piece to the managing editor.

"What do you think?"

"What I said didn't sink in. You need to be easier on the police."

"Easier? Weber is dead because of an inept officer. The Valley Killer is still roaming free because of an inept department. Why should I be easy on them? Don't forget, I may be next." Steve's voice became louder and louder with each sentence.

He walked in circles, wringing his hands and rubbing his head. Fear was fully flowing through the folds of his brain and taking over his body.

The managing editor listened and watched Steve's nerves get the better of him. "Perhaps you're right this time. I like the moniker, 'Valley Killer.' We'll run it on the front page and see what happens. I urge you to take some time off."

"Okay. You're right. I'd like to leave the office before it gets dark."

"Good, good, want someone to ride with you?"

"No, I can handle it."

Steve called a cab, quickly entered, and hunkered down. The ride seemed longer than usual, but he made it home safely—this time.

ℰℛℰℛ

Junior waited on his front lawn for traffic to dissipate before crossing Meyersville Road. He didn't want to be seen. He entered the woods that bordered Mazur's house, walked till he could not see the road, and sought out a strong sapling. Finding a sturdy one in a small clearing, he chopped it down with an axe, settled crossed legged on the leaf and moss covered ground, and began to whittle one end into a sharp point with a single blade Schrade pocket knife. Cutting off the top of the maple, he now had a crude five foot spear. Creeping to the end of the woods, he looked for cars and, finding none, ran across the road and quickly went inside his house.

This would be so enjoyable and so confusing to the police. In addition, he hoped Mazur would become deathly frightened.

Junior tested the point again for sharpness and practiced a series of air thrusts—and then on a whole watermelon in the stained chipped bathroom tub. It felt so satisfying when the point punctured the rind and entered the meaty part. It was exciting as the red juice leaked from the wounds.

This lasted the rest of the afternoon till the melon was in pieces too small to spear.

ೋ

Teddy Nestor couldn't sleep. He tried to understand what was happening. Dingy sheets had been kicked off the bed as he struggled with thoughts pounding throughout his head.

A damp flat pillow only added to the night's depression.

All the recent deaths centering on Troop 186 finally had an adverse effect on him. His environment had changed after years of adjustment and control. Teddy hated change. The good his medicine provided and the calm professional counseling were being eroded. People he knew were dying. He suspected Gary Wilton Senior, but was afraid to bring this suspicion to anyone's attention. No one had ever listened to him. Gary had a rough life that included a childhood filled with punishment and grief, and while Teddy knew the jokes and jabs of the Troop were not intentionally harmful even though they hurt, Gary never felt that way. He took everything personally and Biblically criminal. The Troop had been a community Teddy fit into, regardless of its maliciousness. With the exception of occasional camaraderie with himself and Johnny, Gary was a loner. Gary could be dangerous.

Teddy gazed at the ceiling illuminated by the street light and nightstand lamp. He lightly dragged his fingers up and down his stomach, hoping to relax and concentrate. The cracks and flaking paint were familiar, but similar to clouds, he could always pick out different shapes and patterns. Tonight he didn't like what he saw. He had to tell someone of his thoughts. Maybe Mazur. Not the police. He wouldn't survive interrogation and would become confused. He hated confusion more than anything. Something needed to be done before Mazur was killed, but would the killing stop there?

"Am I safe?" Teddy spoke to the uncaring ceiling. The lamp was turned off and with these final words Teddy slipped into a long restless sleep.

ℰℐℰℐ

It was after midnight when Junior hid his car in the Metzer's Meats and Deli back parking lot off Main Avenue. He wore his darkest clothes and a knit cap to hold his hair in place. As before, he used latex gloves and stretched black athletic socks over his canvas sneakers to muffle footprints.

Junior tested the point of the watermelon stained maple lance. It was still sharp.

As he started out, the moon was hidden by clouds, but pale light filtered through them, so stealthy walking behind the hardware, barber, boutique shops, and abandoned structures lining Main was possible without bumping into trash containers or falling because of potholes. Junior approached the corner of Main and Essex Street and turned left into the backyards of the factory houses. His ride-bys the day before didn't reveal any outside dogs that might cause disturbances. He silently moved in a low crouch, the spear in his right arm pointing the way. All the houses were dark—their occupants sleeping, unaware of the nearby shadowy figure that floated behind trees, sheds, bushes, and around fences. Junior spotted the covered, broken-down motorcycle and green Galaxie marking Teddy's house. He sat in the backyard on an upturned old tin bucket in an old weed-infested vegetable garden savoring the event to come. The anticipation of danger, the hiding, and watching were intoxicating. He remembered Calhoun's closet, deep inside, hearing footsteps approaching his lair. Next to the actual taking of life, this wait was almost orgasmic.

This kill was as necessary as the others. He knew his father would approve. He knew God would approve: Thessalonians 1:6, "Since indeed God considers it just to repay with affliction those who afflict you."

Teddy could afflict him and would if he knew. This was the right and just thing to do.

Junior moved quickly and quietly to the back door, careful to avoid the street lamp light. From his shirt pocket, he took out a square strip of plastic cut from a soda bottle. With skills he had learned before finding the path of righteousness, he slid the plastic between the old door and jamb at a perpendicular angle. He titled the plastic left and pushed, then bent the strip to the right. It slipped under the aged angled end of the door bolt, forcing it back into the door. Leaning against the door, he popped it open.

He was in the kitchen. Darkness was translucent allowing shadows to exist. The house was quiet. Emptiness made its existence known through bare floors and minimal furniture. Junior carefully walked to the next room, using his spear as a cane, lightly searching out the silhouettes ahead of him. The athletic socks dampened his footsteps as he entered the living room. Vacant. His heart was racing. The street lamp shed a pale light through the curtained windows. Carefully, he climbed the wooden stairs, testing each riser for any squeaks before stepping on it. Two doors were on the second floor to the right. The first was not locked. Cautiously, he pushed it in. The room smelled stale, unused. A made bed, dresser, and side table wrapped in layers of dust—nothing else. Junior stopped outside and turned to the next door, gathering calm and composure. This had to be Teddy's bedroom. Slowly he turned the door knob and opened the entrance just enough to peer in.

Teddy was lying on his back in bed, covers thrown off. His right arm began to jerk and he muttered something. Junior ducked behind the door, thinking he was awake. Waiting for a few minutes, he again looked inside. Teddy was dreaming and, like a dog, his body reacted to his thoughts. The light from outside was dim, but it was enough to navigate the room. Junior crept to the side of the bed and raised his spear. His plan was a deep stab in the throat to prevent any vocalization then several in the midsection. Teddy moved again, startling Junior. He stepped back and bumped into an old nightstand. An involuntary "Damn!" came out. The spear knocked against the stand leg.

"What?" Teddy questioned the room sleepily, his eyelids struggling to open.

Junior rushed forward and thrust the tip into Teddy's throat. The point slid off the tough cartilage of the Adam's apple and only grazed the neck.

Teddy grabbed his neck. "Hey!"

As Teddy turned to sit up, Junior drove the maple spike into his midsection.

Teddy's eyes were wide open. Surprise, puzzlement, and pain smothered any desire to fight back.

Another stab then more, forcing Teddy back on the bed. Junior liked the feel from the tautness of the skin before it popped: similar to biting into a Coney Island hotdog.

Teddy began a low moan, clutching his stomach. Junior tried the throat again. He held Teddy's head and placed the tip below the protruding Adam's apple. Pushing with one hand, he forced the stick into the throat. With this entry point established, Junior succeeded in punching a raw hole to the larynx with the strength of two hands.

Teddy grabbed his neck with his right hand. The left still massaged a wet mass, which looked like red pieces of watermelon. Blood filled the ragged holes and flowed onto the bed, slowly seeping into the mattress. When Junior pulled the spear out, blood poured through Teddy's fingers. His eyes were wide with incomprehension and, as he tried to vocalize, pink bubbles formed in the spaces around his hand. Teddy was getting cold and felt no pain. He stared at the ceiling. The cracks were the frowns and snarls of the Troop mocking him one last time. He didn't deserve this. The past was gone forever now. Teddy left as confused as he had been so many years ago. It finally was time to move on.

Junior was in a frenzy, breathing hard, spittle oozing from the corners of his mouth. He continued the attack till all tension was released from Teddy. He rested, watching for any signs of life. Teddy's eyes never closed. Moving to the other side of the bed, above Teddy's head, Junior raised the spear one more time and brought it forcefully down left of the breastbone, hoping it entered the heart. He released his grip and the lance remained upright. Stepping back, he admired his work. This brutality would provide additional fame for the Valley Killer and ensure his safety, since it didn't conform to any previous murders.

Junior looked around the room for a mirror and found none. On a quick visual inspection of his clothes and shoes, he didn't find any trace of Teddy.

Outside, he sat on the tin bucket waiting for the shakes that usually came after a kill. The night had been his. He was a force to be reckoned with. He had the power. He could choose anyone in the neighborhood. He was God's avenger!

Stealthy, he backtracked. At the car, he opened the trunk and retrieved a plastic bag. Junior removed the gloves, athletic socks, his shirt, and pants, and placed them in the bag, along with two bricks. Taking fresh clothes from the back seat, he dressed. Junior drove past his house, around Meyersville Center to Meyersville Road and into the swamp. At the first bridge, he slowed making sure he was alone on the road. Taking the tied bag, he threw it into the murky black water and watched it sink. He then went home to bathe in diluted bleach water to remove any blood spatter on his skin.

e/ɔe/ɔ

A bay was finally empty. Jason Blewett carefully drove the Chrysler 300 in. He viewed the car front to back. He opened the hood. The fact that Junior drove her meant the engine may only need a tune up—all original components appeared to be there. Sure some corrosion and dents, a needed paint job, and interior work, but he was equipped for this. Jason couldn't imagine Junior's lack of foresight. This would be a fun project to work on and perhaps make thousands. He walked across the bay to his office to finish his warm coffee and read the *Newark Star Ledger* newspaper he had bought several days ago, but hadn't found the time to enjoy. Positioning his desk chair so that he could look through the open door at his new acquisition, Jason took a sip and began to read.

Sports first. Even though he knew the scores by now, the commentaries were always interesting. Next the comics, and finally a scan of the news. There had been an accident on South Orange Avenue. One sentence stood out about a gray car with large tail fins. Jason folded the newspaper on his lap and stared at the Chrysler 300 then reread the article.

He walked around the car looking for damage—nothing. The glove box was empty—no registration. Then he noticed the vehicle identification number had been removed from the dashboard. Jason checked the engine block, car frame, rear wheel well, and drive-side doorjamb—all the VIN plates were gone. This was unprecedented. Someone wanted the 300 to be untraceable. More important, without the number, Jason couldn't sell it in its present state much less repaired to original condition.

Back at his desk, he reread the accident article for a third time then picked up the telephone.

ഇ൭ഇ൭

All the curtains and blinds were drawn in Steve's house so he wouldn't be visible. Periodically, he would peer out a window, but fear took hold and he closed the curtains or drew the blinds. He had noticed patrol cars driving by more frequently, but no one guarded the back of the house. Steve hadn't shaved or slept much. The false protection of being a reporter fell apart with Peter's death. The killer was persistent and Steve was the last scout. He thought about going to his in-laws and being with his wife and kids, but the killer might follow him. He couldn't risk that. Steve paced through empty rooms, asking questions but finding no answers.

e∕ɔe∕ɔ

Lieutenant Arnold scanned all the reports on his desk about the recent murders: all were members of the same Scout Troop. Nothing else. There had to be another connection. Interviews with neighbors, friends, and even acquaintances didn't provide any leads.

Township residents were alarmed and frightened. Mazur didn't help matters, only exasperated them. Secretly and guiltily, Arnold wished Mazur was next. Every officer was reminded of the murders at every roll call. Sergeant Molosic was put back on active patrol. Arnold needed all boots on the ground.

Without creditable leads, he was forced to ask for help, an action he construed as weakness.

The lieutenant called the State Trooper Violent Crime Analysis Unit and accepted their help. He had no choice. The unit had sources his department didn't have or could afford. The unit would forward its finding to the FBI National Center for the Analysis of Violent Crime. The center provided behavioral based investigation for repetitive violent crimes. The motivation of the Valley Killer would hopefully be known soon. There was always a clue, always a lead, but for now they were hidden. The killer was bound to make a mistake, but how many more lives would it take for this to happen?

⋐⋑⋐⋑

The euphoria Gary Junior experienced on this last kill had disappeared and he could not summon it back, even when he remembered the tension snap of the spear point into Teddy's soft stomach. Two to go, but he felt it was time now to tell his father what he had done for him. He needed his father's blessing and praise.

Junior drove to the Salvation Army in Morristown. Parking on Spring Street, he walked up the sloping sidewalk to the back of the headquarters. Both bay doors were closed. Junior tried the entry door between the bays. It was open. It took a while for his eyes to adjust from the bright early morning light to the muted interior. A pair of white Dodge vans with the distinctive red Salvation Army shield were parked inside. A green Volvo was wedged between the two. On his left in the corner was a small wooden bench with a work light.

"Dad?"

No response.

Near the work bench was another door. It was closed. Junior knocked. Knocked again then tried the door knob. It turned and Junior stepped into the room. His father was sleeping on a cot.

"Dad?"

Gary turned toward the voice, trying to remember where he was. "What?"

"Dad!"

"Junior?"

"Yes, I've come to visit and tell you some wondrous news. Something I've done that will make your day, and that will make up for everything."

"Oh?" Gary rubbed his eyes slowly becoming awake. "What is it?"

"I've avenged you."

"You did what?" Gary was now sitting, looking at Junior, trying to follow the conversation.

"Let me put it this way, Exodus 21:24-25. 'Eye for eye, tooth for tooth, hand for hand, foot for foot, burn for burn, wound for wound, stripe for stripe.'"

"What are you talking about?"

"I mean I've avenged you!" Junior broke out in a big smile and raised his arms in supplication. Psalm 94:1. 'O Lord, God of vengeance, O God of vengeance, shine forth!'"

"Avenged me?"

"Yes, I got rid of most of those who once humiliated you."

"I'm still not following you son."

"I am the Valley Killer!" Junior announced and

reached out for the hug he knew was coming.

"You're the Valley Killer? You murdered all those men?" Gary was now completely awake, though what he was hearing did not seem real.

"I did it for you, Dad! I did it for me! I avenged the wrongs done to you in your past and all those times I had to hear about them." Junior kept his arms wide, waiting.

"You idiot! What have you done?"

Junior was shocked by Gary's response. "I'm killing off Troop 186! I'm doing it for you. You don't understand. I did it for you, Dad. For us. For our family honor."

Though the area was small, Gary found room to stand and began pacing, ignoring the visible plea for gratitude from his son. "Oh, oh, I understand well enough now. You're, you're worse than they ever were! They teased and bullied. They never killed! You're the worst tyrant."

"What do you mean? I delivered the justice they deserved!" Junior was beginning to lose some of his certainty.

"Nobody deserves death, nobody! You have it all wrong. You want to quote the Bible? Romans 12:19, 'Beloved, never avenge yourselves, but leave it to the wrath of God, for it is written, Vengeance is mine, I will repay, says the Lord.' *You* are not God!"

"No. No!" Junior lowered his arms and stood incredulously. This was not supposed to happen.

"What you did was wrong, wrong! Harmful acts aren't always intentional. A life is worth so much more than a boyish insult. You, you—" Gary couldn't verbally express his shock and so shook his fists in frustration.

"But it affected you for so long and I had to hear about it for all these years!"

"Sure, it did. But to kill over it is completely wrong, it's a Cardinal sin! You turned into one of them, only worse. You're a murderer! It's my fault, all my fault. What did I do to you? I'm just like they were!"

"I did it for you, Daddy, for you!" Tears visibility welled in Junior's eyes.

Gary was irate as well as saddened, uncertain what to do. Why did Junior tell him? "You're an idiot! A killer, a serial killer—my own son!" Gary pushed him aside as he walked toward the door, trying to get some separation to think.

The repeated word "idiot" formed a three-dimensional image in Junior's head. Each line of the word grew like sausages expanding on a hot grill constricting other thoughts. *Idiot.* "What, what are you going to do?"

"I don't know. I don't know!"

"Who are you going to tell? You're going to tell someone, aren't you?"

"Tell?'

"Yes, you're going to tell someone what I did, aren't you? You're going to tell Teddy or Giovanni, or worse the police!" Junior grabbed his head to contain the explosion of rage brought on by the image.

Gary shrugged his shoulders, unsure of what to do. He needed to distance himself from this person he had called son. He needed to think.

Junior read the shrug as a "Yes." The pictograph burst. He lunged forward and grabbed Gary from behind in a choke hold. "I did this for you! For you! *For you!*"

Gary tried to fight back, but Junior was on top of him squeezing harder and harder. They fell to the hard floor, rolling and grunting. Junior pinned him down face up and began to apply pressure with thumbs to the carotid artery. Gary reached out for anything and found his Bible. He pounded the book on Junior's left temple. Junior hit Garry's arm and the Bible flew under the cot its pages opened. On the exposed page was Exodus 20:13. *You shall not kill.*

Gary tried to wretch Junior's hands from his neck and then started to beat him around the face with his fists. Junior sat upright on Gary's stomach, his longer reach out-distancing Gary's shorter arms.

"You made my life miserable by telling and retelling me about your pathetic childhood. I wanted to end it."

Junior felt the blood flow gradually diminishing. He constricted the flesh harder now, not from anger but with experienced pleasure. He breathed in another life. Long after Gary stopped moving, Junior continued till his hands began to cramp. He moved off the still body and rested on the floor. He tried to be sad that his father was dead, but the thrill of the kill blocked that emotion. Besides, his father had been more than ungrateful. He was completely selfish and insensible. After subjecting him time and time again to the stories of the boyhood injustices received from the Troop that was, at times, unbearable. He actually was going to the police. Now, after what he went through, all the planning and all the risks to be so unappreciated, it just wasn't right. It wasn't right! This man actually favored those who hurt him over his own son. Junior looked at the body but didn't see his father anymore.

After the shakes came and went, he became more professional. Since this hadn't been planned, he needed to think and act quickly. What to do with the body. Stage a hanging suicide? Set fire to it in the Volvo? In the end, Junior decided to leave it where it was. Perhaps the police would attribute the murder to a robbery. If they linked it to the Valley Killer, all the better. No one would suspect a son of killing his father. Junior carefully went through the room making sure no evidence was left behind. He found a dirty towel and wiped the door knob then peaked out the bay entrance door. No one was around. Wiping both inside and outside knobs, he quickly walked back to his car, folding the dingy towel and concealing it the best he could with his hands. His face throbbed with bruises and scratch marks. He would lay low till the discoloration faded away and the abrasions healed.

Junior drove home with renewed certainty in his work. He had plans to create. His mission wasn't complete, even though the reason for it no longer existed.

❧❦❧

Giovanni hadn't heard from Gary or Teddy. The newspaper was quiet about the Valley Killer. Even patrons of the Stirling Inn didn't mention the murders. It was as if silence would somehow make the killer disappear. They were frightened, though. The Inn cleared out before dark. Even the regulars left in the "safety" of the sun. They had already forgotten that most of the deaths occurred during the day.

With the afternoon off, Giovanni decided to walk to Teddy's house to see if anything was new. He wasn't afraid. His membership in the Troop was brief and no one had cared about him before. Why should they now?

Main Avenue was almost deserted. The commuter train wasn't due at the Stirling Station for another hour and shopping had been concentrated at the malls. The town was dead but didn't know it. Proprietors heard footsteps and looked out windows and doors, anticipating a customer as Giovanni walked past the deli, barber, hardware, and boutique shops. They were used to disappointment and returned to magazines or soap operas as he continued on.

He turned left on Essex Street and, not for the first

time, viewed all the same white houses on either side, thinking what a great puzzle the scene would make. Counting the houses, he stopped at number nineteen and looked for the covered motorcycle to make sure he was correct. No response to his knocks. He knocked again while trying to see through the grimy window near the door.

Teddy must be working. Giovanni headed back to the Inn.

e/se/s

It seemed the night was hemorrhaging the color it had trapped from the day. Red, blue, and white pulsed through the front window blinds.

Steve didn't hear any sirens, but as he peeked out, as he had habitually done now, he saw Township and state trooper cars speed by.

It appeared to him they were stopping at Gary's house.

Throwing caution to the wind, knowing law enforcement was nearby, Steve nervously walked up Meyersville Road. He was right, Gary's house had all the lamps on inside and was bathed in white light outside from patrol car spot lights. Police, troopers, and suited men rushed in and around the house and yard.

Steve approached Lieutenant Arnold on the front lawn. When the lieutenant was finished speaking into a shoulder microphone, Steve asked, "What's going on here?"

Arnold turned, took a minute to look at Steve. "Well I suppose you should know. This morning a call came from the Howell Township Police about a gray car with large fins—the type described by witnesses at Weber's death. The owner of a junk yard said that Gary Wilton Junior dropped it off to be crushed. The vehicle identification plates were all removed. We came here for answers, but Junior wasn't home so we went to see his father. We found him dead."

"Dead?"

"Apparently strangled. But we also found matter under his fingernails and blood on the spine of a Bible. We rushed the evidence and samples from the father to be analyzed. It turns out that the initial testing proved the DNA from the fingernails and Bible were a near match to Gary Junior. And that led us here. Gary Wilton Junior is a prime suspect."

"Gary Wilton Junior! Why would he kill his father?"

"We don't know the motive yet, but every indication leads to the kid. As for you, you best go home or we can place you in protective custody. The killer is still loose and apparently close to you."

"Wouldn't Junior run for it?"

"Who knows? You're the last of the Troop. What do you want to do?"

"I'll take protective custody."

"Good move, I'll have an officer drive you home to collect your stuff. For now you can be safe in jail."

∽∾∽

Junior had gone for a slice of pizza at the Stirling Inn as an excuse to visit Giovanni. He didn't like loose ends. Giovanni could still cause him problems, somehow. He was convinced of that. After this task, Mazur would end this current mission. Giovanni brought a tray of clean glasses to the bar and gave a nod of recognition to Junior.

Gulping down the last of his Diet Coke, Junior went to the kitchen. Giovanni was at the stainless steel sink, washing dinner dishes and flatware.

"Johnny!"

Giovanni looked up and smiled, happy that Junior came back to see him. He was glad to have any visitor. "Junior! How are you?"

"Fine, how are you doing my friend?"

"All right, all right. You know things could be better, but then they always could be, you know?"

"Yeah, I know."

"How's your dad doing?"

"He's at peace."

"Good, good."

"Listen, you want to go to a movie?"

"Movie?"

"Yeah, I thought it would be good for you to get out.

Take your mind away from work and all this other business."

"Well…"

"Come on, it'll be good for you and for me."

"Could we invite Teddy?"

"He's working nights."

"Ah, I went to see him. He probably was sleeping."

"Yeah, he's sleeping. How about tomorrow night?"

"Sure. What time?"

"Let's get a late show, say around eight to give us time to travel to Morristown. You want to see anything in particular?"

"Something light."

"Okay, I'll look in the papers. I'll pick you up. See you then."

Junior left to flesh out his plan. He knew he would dump Johnny's body in the swamp. Watching his clothes submerge in the murky water spawned the idea. Just how to kill remained in question. He had run out of creative ideas. The meeting tonight with Johnny added a delightful layer. He never spoke with his quarry before a killing. Knowing that their death was coming was exceptionally enjoyable.

The glow of the pulsating lights was noticeable well before he came near the house. He didn't slow down. Peripherally viewing the scene, he could make out police and state troopers patrol cars and a great deal of officials walking around. He must have made a mistake somewhere! Junior pounded on the steering wheel with his right fist. What was it? He had been so careful. Now he had to improvise. Johnny wasn't a threat anymore now, but Mazur was the end to his God-given assignment to punish these bullies.

Since the law probably knew he was the Valley Killer now, there was no need to be secret. Junior was relieved and excited. People would know his name and he would bring awareness to this long-ignored bullying condition. He would be famous!

Parking in the Meyersville Presbyterian Church lot, Junior skulked along the road side toward his house, turned at a forty-five degree angle into the wet woods, and quietly headed to the junk yard, careful of fallen logs and thorn bushes. The bright spot lights and patrol flashers filtered through the trees and helped illuminate the way. Junior kept to the fringe of the colorful lights. He could hear the noise of talk on the lawn. Even being careful, he stepped on several dead branches. The cracking caught the attention of the police. Junior hunkered down.

"What was that?"

"Probably deer."

"Well, shine the spot light over there."

The light produced shadows and nothing else.

"I'll go look." An officer headed toward the woods but stopped short of entering it. It was overgrown, creepy, and swampy. He made a show of searching then retreated back to the lawn.

Junior bent low and continued Indian-style, placing the toe of a foot first then slowly resting the heel.

At the edge of the tree line bordering the junk yard, Junior stopped and observed. No one was searching the yard. They were probably waiting for dawn. He made his way along the dirt paths, aided by the spill off the bright light focused on the house. In the far back where darkness again took over, he made a right by the orange and white Volkswagen bus, then a left by a stack of tires, and found the rear end of a rusted light-green 1954 Buick Century that had been dropped in a thicket of brush. Junior took out his key ring and shielding a pocket flashlight with his body, unlocked the large trunk. Inside was a knapsack with a change of clothes and money. Wrapped in blankets were his .22 scoped rifle and a Chinese Type 56 assault rifle. Checking the forty-round magazine in the automatic weapon, Junior said a thankful pray to the National Rifle Association for its lobbying and narrow reading of the Second Amendment. Strapping on a camouflaged triple magazine pouch and shouldering the assault rifle, he reached for the knapsack, picked it up, thought for a moment, then left it. This indeed was the end and he wouldn't need it. Locking the trunk, he set off back into the woods to Steve's house.

A patrol car was in the driveway. Junior absently patted the brown wooden stock of the Type 56. No need to worry. Moving the select lever to L for fully automatic, he walked to the front door, opened it and spotted an officer standing in the living room looking out the side window. Junior leveled the assault rifle and squeezed the trigger.

Nerves and the initial kick back threw his aim off. The wall behind the officer became perforated with black holes. Startled, the officer turned then reached for his 9 mm handgun. Before he could remove it from its holster, Junior gained control and diagonally riddled the officer's midsection. His body collapsed and he fell forward, hitting an upholstered chair before sliding onto the floor. Junior replaced the magazine.

"Steve!" he called, "Steve, where are you?"

Upstairs he heard a door close. Taking two steps at a time, he reached the second floor. Flashes of Teddy came back as he tried each door in the hall. All the rooms were empty. He could hear the cars coming down the road. Time was important now. Inspecting the largest room at the end of the hall again, he now noticed a suitcase on the bed. Scraping and whimpering came from the walk-in closet. Junior quickly opened the door. It slammed against the wall and started to shut again. Placing a foot to stop the door, Junior peered inside.

Steve was huddled in the corner, fear masking his weeping face.

"What, what do you want with me?"

"This." Junior brought the rifle up from his side and emptied the clip. Steve was almost cut in half. His upper body seemed to slide to the left. The iron smell of blood and the distinctive order of feces permeated the closet.

The distinguishing sound of automatic firing in the still night had galvanized the law enforcement throng outside Junior's house. Some came by car. Others ran as fast as they could to the Mazur residence.

Junior stepped through the opened front door. Cars disgorged excited men with drawn pistols and aimed rifles. More came up the drive and hid behind the cars. Shotguns were cocked and sighted. Car spot lights blinded him.

"Put the weapon down!" Lieutenant Arnold yelled and then repeated as a megaphone was placed in his hand.

Junior surveyed the commotion. This would have to be the end of his task. Johnny was just lucky. Fame now waited. New Jersey didn't have a death penalty. Compared to his present environment, three meals a day, a warm bed, and the respect of inmates for his deeds would be welcomed. Junior felt compelled to proclaim his mission, to explain that harmful acts were always intentional and had wide repercussions across the years and across families. He was carrying out God's word.

From behind an open patrol car door, Sergeant Molosic stared intently at the Type 56 assault rifle Junior held against his leg. He realized that Junior probably bought it on a run to Pennsylvania and that Junior might use information about illegal arms trafficking to mediate his sentencing somehow.

Molosic's involvement and Don Gold's death would place him in a cell next to Junior.

Junior raised his arms to heaven, forgetting the left one held the rifle. He formed the Scout sign with his right fingers. "Jeremiah 9:9 'Avenge me on my persecutors.' You see before you the Valley Killer enforcing God's law!"

As Junior reached up to the Lord, Molosic yelled out, "He's going to shoot! He's going to shoot!" The sergeant knew the warning couldn't be traced back to him in the heat and excitement of the event.

Township Police were aware that one of them had been in the house and they knew now that Junior was the serial killer.

Without hesitation, fire erupted from a few, and then all of the officers discharged their weapons.

"Stop shooting! Stop!" Arnold's words were cut into pieces by the flying lead and never heard.

The lieutenant and Molosic didn't shoot. The sergeant didn't want to develop a pattern following Gold's death. The lieutenant just knew better.

Junior was engulfed in a storm of bullets, ripping open his face and chest. He was dead before what was left of his body slumped outside the door. Police and state troopers rushed past the oozing mound of flesh into the house to discover the fate of those inside. Molosic looked down on Junior and muttered, "Moron. Why did I do business with white trash?"

Motivation for the Township killings by Gary Wilton Junior was never determined. Mental illness was settled on for convenience.

෧෩෧

The land had become scarred with more people and developments, but hosted these parasites with dignity. The Township grew and healed, forgetting the killings all too soon out of necessity. Life tenuously moved on till another disruption occurred. This was the process.

A weather worn cedar shake bungalow occupied a small area on the slope of 13 Lacey Avenue in Homestead Park. Yellow light escaping from a single side window tried to penetrate into the late summer evening but was defused outside by a weak rain.

A thin lonely figure huddled over a chipped laminated desk, caressing old newspaper clippings neatly arranged in a worn paper scrap book. An index finger traced the path of each sentence, occasionally pushing eyeglasses back to the bridge of the nose. This had become almost a nightly ritual after experiencing another day of silent suffering.

It had been a particularly humiliating day. He didn't look forward to tomorrow. Slowly, he reread the outdated articles about the Valley Killer. He was fascinated by the ingenious methods of dispatch.

He was hopeful because of the success Gary Wilton

Junior achieved before his journey's end. There could be relief!

Not for the first time he wondered what it was like to give the gift of death. How would he kill? Who he would kill was an easy question. When?

About the Author

Mr. Milos was a Boy Scout residing in Meyersville, New Jersey. Now living in Brunswick, New York, his career has included teaching English as foreign language with the Peace Corps in Afghanistan, public school English teacher, and professional positions in communication and documentation. He has published two books: *The Kush, Strings,* and a novella: *Miles from Millersburg.*